Courtyard Cat

by *C. S. Adler*

Clarion Books
New York

Clarion Books
a Houghton Mifflin Company imprint
215 Park Avenue South, New York, NY 10003
Text copyright © 1995 by Carole S. Adler

Type is 12.5/15.5-point Caslon 540

Printed in the USA.

Library of Congress Cataloging-in-Publication Data
Adler, C. S. (Carole S.)
Courtyard cat / by C. S. Adler.
p. cm.
Summary: Eleven-year-old Lindsay blames herself for the accident
to her brother which forced her family to move to a city where she feels
uncomfortable and friendless.
ISBN 0-395-71126-6
[1. Brothers and sisters—Fiction. 2. City and town life—Fiction.
3. Guilt—Fiction. 4. Cats—Fiction. 5. Friendship—Fiction.] I. Title.
PZ7.A26145Co 1996
[Fic]—dc20   94-22179
CIP
AC

BP 10 9 8 7 6 5 4 3 2 1

To Steve and Karen,
and a long, joyful life together.

chapter

1

"Why wouldn't you talk to your friend when she phoned, Lindsay?" Mama was dressed in her postal worker's uniform, bruise-blue pants and shirt, ready to leave for her new job here in Schenectady.

Lindsay shrugged her slim shoulders and dropped her eyes to keep Mama from reading them. "Rona said she thinks you're mad at her or something," Mama persisted.

"I'm not. I just don't want to talk to her now." Lindsay never had known how to put words to her feelings, and lately she felt so bad she had no words, not even for her first and best friend.

She ran her eyes around the living room of the new apartment. It looked dim as an old cave lived in by too many people for too many years. The kitchen was so tiny that Dad had had to put their kitchen table in the living room. He'd jammed the

TV set, couch, and one easy chair into the remaining space.

Mama's deep brown eyes had followed Lindsay's. "Well," Mama said, flipping her long hair back nervously, "I know you're not too pleased with this place, but we have to make the best of it until your father finishes his computer service training thing and finds a job."

"I know."

Mama's lips worked in her thin face as if she were searching for something comforting to say to Lindsay, but Mama had no talent for words either. Finally she gave up and said simply, "You keep a sharp eye on Garth, now. Don't let him get out of the courtyard. The street's not safe."

"I know," Lindsay repeated. She had seen the overflowing garbage cans at the curb beside the stream of truck and car traffic—also the teenagers boldly eyeing her family's belongings while Dad and his friends were unloading the rented moving van and Dad's old pickup truck this past weekend.

"The landlady says her other tenants use the courtyard like a mini-park," Mama said hopefully. "No other apartment we saw had a yard. And Garth needs to get outside some. You can handle him, can't you, Lindsay?" Mama's eyes worried at her from dark hollows. "Taking care of a three-year-old all day's a big responsibility, and Garth's willful, but when I was your age, I had to nurse my sick mama. You've always been so good at handling things, Lindsay." Mama looked close to tears.

"It's okay, Mama. I can do it." The words came out confident. They sounded like the old Lindsay, the way she'd been before Garth's accident.

Mama nodded with relief and glanced at her watch. "I better go or I'll be late." She drew Lindsay's thin, elastic body to her and hugged her. "I know I can count on you. I know that," Mama said before she left.

The words curled softly around Lindsay. She had once been proud that she could be counted on. "I can do it," she had said, so often that Daddy called her the can-do girl. But now she'd changed. Somehow it had gotten hard to do anything.

She went to the bedroom she shared with her brother. Garth was still asleep, buried under the covers so that only his tousled golden curls showed. She raised the shade over the barred window that protected them from passersby on the sidewalk just outside and was met by an old man's startled gaze. Instantly she lowered the shade and the forest-green walls closed in around her again.

She got out the animal posters she'd taken from her big, light corner bedroom in Schuylerville. In their rented farmhouse there, the windows collected sunshine from surrounding fields full of milkweed and daisies and buttercups. Hard to believe that it was only an hour from Schuylerville to this sad old

3

industrial city in upstate New York. Well, the posters would brighten the room some.

As Lindsay began taping them to the walls, her leg brushed against Garth's toy box. He played indoors only on rainy days. Mostly he liked to be outside digging. "Never saw such a kid for digging," Dad always said when he came upon one of Garth's impressive excavations. She'd get out Garth's pail and shovel and take him outside as soon as he woke up.

The phone rang. Lindsay was tempted not to answer it. But she knew she'd better. It might be the doctor about scheduling one of the operations Garth needed.

"Lindsay . . ." Jill's nasal voice was excited as usual. "Rona says you're mad at her."

"I'm not."

"Well, why wouldn't you talk to her when she called?"

"I just got here this weekend. I don't have anything to say."

"Oh, Lindsay!" Jill sounded disgusted. "Listen, Rona and I are going shopping for your birthday and I need to know what you want."

"Whatever you get will be fine. Anyway, we can talk about it when you and Rona come Saturday."

"Yeah, well, now my big brother says he can't drive us this weekend. Can your folks bring you back here instead?"

4

"I don't think so."

Jill and Rona had promised they weren't going to lose touch just because Lindsay was moving an hour away. "We'll still be best friends," Rona had said. And now Jill was going shopping with Rona, Jill who had everything—a horse of her own and a barn with a rope to swing on. For a whole year Jill had pried apart Lindsay and Rona's twosome. She'd made it a threesome that she could fit into. Now, with Lindsay gone, Rona wouldn't have anything better to do than ride Jill's horse, or play in her barn, or fish in her pond. "An hour isn't so far away," Mama had said, but already Lindsay could see that it was.

Jill rattled on, "You'll never believe what happened to me, Lindsay. I lost the sapphire from the ring my grandma gave me."

"That's too bad."

"Grandma'll *kill* me when she finds out."

"Didn't you say the ring was old? Probably the stone was loose and it wasn't your fault."

"You're right! That's what I'll tell her. Thanks, Lindsay. I guess Rona's right. You are smart. Well, it's long-distance so I better say 'bye. You call me back soon, okay?"

"Jill," Lindsay said quickly, "please tell Rona I'm not mad at her."

Lindsay put down the receiver feeling as if she were caught in a vise. She was still standing beside the kitchen wall phone, wondering if she should call Rona back without anything good to tell her, when Garth poked his face around the corner. "Boo!" he said.

"Boo, yourself." Lindsay smiled affectionately at her brother, but a shudder went through her. His face still did that to her when she saw it suddenly. Even though the accident had happened in April and now it was July, Garth's ruined mouth still shocked her with its twisted lips and crisscrossing of scars. Angel face, Mama had called him before the accident. Now the contrast between the beauty of his blue eyes and broad, fair forehead and the lower half of his face made the damage seem all the more terrible.

"Want Oaty Oats for breakfast, Garth?" she asked him.

"No, pizza."

"Cereal's what we have. Oaty Oats or flakes?" Lindsay said.

"No," he said. His eyes challenged her as if they were playing a game, but it wasn't a game for her. The way he resisted her now made her chest tight. He used to listen. He used to obey her the way he obeyed their parents. But ever since the accident, he'd changed.

"You go watch TV. I'll bring your breakfast to you there," Lindsay told him.

"Okay," he said because that was a treat. Mama didn't let him eat in front of the TV. He padded to the set, barefoot in his rocket-printed pajamas, and turned it on. Lindsay fixed a bowl of cereal for him which he ate with his eyes six inches from the cartoon animals on the screen. When she pulled him back a foot, the way Mama always did, he kept spooning up the cereal.

Through the living room window, Lindsay saw something move in the tree in the center of the courtyard. A cat? She ran to open the window and leaned out as the slinky, brownish body disappeared into the thick leaves. If the cat lived here, maybe she could make friends with it, Lindsay thought. She'd take it some milk when she went outside with Garth.

The courtyard wasn't very big, about the size of a swimming pool. The building surrounded it on three sides. Two apartments, one on top of the other, looked into it from one side and two from the other. A two-story lobby connected the apartments in the middle. In it were the doors to the ground floor apartments, plus staircases to each of the two upstairs apartments.

An iron fence with a gate in it ran across the front of the courtyard. Just inside the fence grew a thick, high hedge of yew that blocked off the view of the side street. The hedge was what made the courtyard seem safe, Lindsay thought, even though the latch on the gate was broken so anyone who wanted to could get in.

She blinked. There was the cat again, but a cat

like none she'd ever seen. Amazing blue eyes, as blue as Garth's, peered at her from a branch of the tree. This cat had perky ears and a brown mask of a face above a deliciously creamy chest. "Here, kitty, here, kitty," Lindsay called hopefully, but the pixie face hid. Only one elegant, sable-tipped leg was still visible, dangling in the air. The little tease!

Cracked concrete blocks made meandering paths between the bare patches of dirt and the corners of the courtyard where ivy grew. A bench stood under the lone tree in the center. Garth could dig in the shade under the tree, Lindsay decided.

"Garth, let's go outside."

"No. I watch my show."

Rather than hassle with him, Lindsay went to their bedroom to unpack her collection of miniature stuffed bears and set them out on her dresser top. She'd won a prize at the county fair last summer for those bears. They were costumed, and she'd made every costume herself as a 4-H project.

The tissue-paper chef's hat had gotten crushed in the box. She blew on the hat gently and set its wearer out among the twenty-four other bears. Rona had helped her with some of their pleated collars, but Jill hadn't helped with any. She was too fidgety to be good with her hands. Lindsay looked at their school pictures, taped to her dresser mirror.

Rona was a tall, sturdy girl with an open, pretty face. Jill looked like a Munchkin, all glasses and grin.

She really should call Rona. Maybe she could tell her about the cat. That would be something good to say about this place.

The TV was still on when Lindsay crossed the living room to get to the phone, but Garth wasn't sitting in front of it. Immediately her heart began racing. Where had he gone? Sometimes he hid just to trick her. Sometimes she pretended to be tricked to make him giggle. But not today. Today she was in charge of him and she had assured her parents she could do it, as if she were still the reliable eleven-year-old of last winter.

Wildly she ran about, looking for him in the bathroom, her parents' bedroom, behind the couch and chair in the living room, and in the cabinet under the sink in the kitchen. "Garth!" she yelled.

The living room window was open—the way she'd left it. Oh, no! Had she done it again? The scene she never quite let herself remember flashed in her mind. "No," she cried and rushed to the open window where once again she screamed out her brother's name.

chapter

2

There was Garth, under the tree, holding the cat which was struggling to get away from him. It cried pathetically and arched its cream-colored belly, scrabbling at the air with its chocolate paws.

"Let go of that animal before it scratches you, boy," an old man said. He was leaning out the window of the ground-floor apartment on the opposite side of the courtyard. Firmly he explained, "Cats don't like being squeezed. Do you hear me?"

"Garth, let go of the kitty," Lindsay called.

Garth turned toward her, his scarred lips twisted in a grotesque smile. "Nice kitty. I pet him," Garth said. Big spade-shaped leaves waved in the breeze over his head and tree roots angled and snaked along the bare ground around his feet. Suddenly the cat dug its claws into Garth's arm. He screamed. The cat squirted from his hands like toothpaste from a tube and was gone over the hedge that shielded the courtyard from the street.

"Mama!" Garth wailed.

"I'll be right there," Lindsay said. The old man left his window, too. Afraid he was on his way to the courtyard to punish Garth for mistreating the cat, Lindsay vaulted the sill. She landed, as Garth must have, on a pile of black plastic bags filled with leaves. She ran to her brother and examined his bleeding arm. Mama had only been gone a few minutes and already they were in the middle of an emergency.

The old man appeared beside Lindsay, leaning on a cane. He had a turtle face with a thin line for a mouth, not much chin, and heavy-lidded eyes. His smooth-skinned face was framed by wispy white hair. "That scratch no doubt looks worse than it is," he said a little breathlessly. "But your mother had best put something on it to keep it from getting infected."

"Mama went to work," Lindsay said.

"Who's taking care of you, then?" the old man asked.

"I'm taking care of Garth. He's my brother," Lindsay said.

"You're young to be in charge." His smile was kind.

Lindsay raised her chin and stood straighter. "I'm eleven," she said. She knew that she looked younger because she was slender and her features were small and indefinite. All she had of Mama's prettiness was the same big brown eyes.

The old man shook his head. He thought a minute before saying, "I suppose what we'll have to do then is take you to my apartment. I've got some antiseptic ointment that ought to do the job."

"No, thank you." Lindsay backed off fast in case the old man was one of those people Mama had warned her against. "I'll take care of it myself."

She began tugging Garth toward the house, but he resisted and pulled loose. "Kitty," he said as he ran toward the gate with the broken latch. Lindsay caught him and lugged him back. Now it was his turn to struggle to get away from her.

"Stop it, Garth. Stop that. You can't go outside. We have to stay in the courtyard. Mama says."

He yanked his arms free and plunked his chunky body onto the ground. "You're mean," he said.

"No, I'm not."

The old man had seated himself on the concrete bench beneath the shade tree. "Would you like me to bring the ointment out here?" he asked.

"Would you please?" Lindsay was embarrassed that he seemed to have understood her suspicions, but she'd rather let him help than have to call Mama at work.

With the aid of his cane, the old man headed

back toward the lobby of the U-shaped building. Lindsay hoped the two upstairs apartments in either wing weren't also occupied by elderly people. In the years before Garth was born, when Mama had had a rural delivery route, Lindsay had been left with a baby-sitting grandmother who'd been young compared to this man. She'd never met anyone as ancient as he seemed.

Just as the old man reached the lobby door, a tall, slim, African-American boy and girl of twelve or thirteen came out. "Hi, Mr. Prior," they said simultaneously. Lindsay wondered if they were twins.

Mr. Prior stopped. "Hello yourselves. Are you off to the playground, Amesley and Anna?"

"Summer program starts today," the boy said. "We're signing up—me for sports and Anna for crafts."

"That sounds like a good way to spend your summer," the old man said. "Have you met our new tenant yet?"

"No. Hi," the girl said to Lindsay. "I'm Anna Blake."

Lindsay introduced herself, but when she turned to tell them her brother's name, she found him busy trying to disentangle the cat from the hedge. It had ventured back into the courtyard too soon.

"Oh-oh, here comes our landlady," the boy called Amesley said. "We got to hide that cat fast."

"You catch her and I'll hide her, Amesley," Mr. Prior said.

Lindsay saw a woman's brassy head with a fancy hairdo bobbing along above the hedge on the street side. The head stopped and a conversation began between the landlady and somebody out on the sidewalk. Meanwhile both Anna and Amesley reached for the cat, which had coiled into a tight, brown lump just beyond Garth's reach.

"Watch out, kid," Amesley hissed at Garth. "We got to save this kitten from the wicked witch before she rips out its claws and tears out its teeth."

"Amesley, get out of the way and stop scaring babies," Anna said. It was she who managed to catch the cat. She presented it to Mr. Prior, who tucked it neatly under his sport jacket and hobbled off into the house.

"So you're the family that just moved in?" Amesley said while the landlady continued her long-time-no-see conversation outside the hedge. "We saw the guys unloading the U-Haul and the pickup. Where you from?"

"Schuylerville," Lindsay said.

"Yeah? Where's that?"

"Out in the country. It's not far." It dismayed her that he hadn't heard of it.

"Bet you already wish you stayed there instead of moving here, huh?" Lindsay smiled and was silent rather than risk being insulting about where Amesley lived. She hadn't known any African

Americans in Schuylerville. In her whole school the only nonwhites had been a couple of Asian kids and once a boy from India for half a term. She liked Amesley's round, open face. He had a neat bush of tight black curls, a wide, flat nose, and eyes as big and brown as her own. His smile was the best thing she'd seen here so far, besides the cat.

"So what happened to your brother's face?" Amesley asked.

Lindsay's smile froze on her lips.

"You're being nosy," Anna told him. She was plainer than the boy, long-faced and solemn.

"Am not," he said. "Am I being nosy?" he asked Lindsay.

"Not really," she mumbled.

"See, Preacher?" he said to Anna.

"What are you two arguing about now?" It was the landlady, who had finally come through the gate into the courtyard. She was tiny and sharp-faced. Her skin hung in wrinkles that made Lindsay guess her to be even older than Mr. Prior despite her yellow-gold hair and her lavender suit and matching high-heeled pumps. "Don't you know twins are supposed to get along? Why are you two always fighting?" she scolded them.

"We're not, Betty. We're just fooling around," Amesley said. "How're you doing?"

"I'm fine. I'm looking for my sister's Siamese cat. Have any of you seen her?"

"That blue-eyed cat? Yeah, she was around here,

15

wasn't she, Anna?" He eyed Garth, who was trying to squeeze into the yew hedge where the cat had been hiding.

"Little boy, you get away from that hedge. You're going to break those branches," the landlady called to Garth. "Who's in charge of that child?" she demanded when Garth ignored her and began snapping off twigs to make the hole bigger.

"Garth, stop that," Lindsay said. She went to pull Garth away from the hedge. He broke loose and crawled under the bench.

"Yeah, you got to watch out for little kids, Betty, especially curly-haired blonds like that one," Amesley said. "He could really trash this yard in no time. Rip the hedge apart with his bare hands, break the stone bench, maybe yank the tree up by its roots."

"My brother's got a warped sense of humor," Anna said to the landlady, who was staring at him openmouthed. "Come on, Amesley, we have to get to the playground before all the good stuff is signed up for."

Amesley turned to Lindsay abruptly and asked, "Why don't you come to the playground with us?"

"I can't," she said. "My mother wants me to keep my little brother in the courtyard."

"Yeah? You're going to have a hard time doing that," Amesley said.

"Let's go." Anna grabbed Amesley's arm and pulled him out the gate into the street.

16

Betty's eyes fell on Garth who was still crouched under the bench. "That child's bleeding," she said, pointing to where the cat had marked his arm. "And what happened to his face?"

Lindsay stiffened. She would never get used to people asking that question. "He had an accident," she said. "Garth, come inside now."

"My goodness," Betty said in alarm. "He didn't get hurt *here*, did he?"

"The cat scratched his arm," Lindsay said. "His face got hurt in April."

"The cat—a Siamese cat?"

"I guess so," Lindsay said.

"Well, I'm sure it was your brother's fault, and you better tell your parents that if they try to sue—"

"Relax, Betty." It was Mr. Prior, hobbling to the rescue with a first-aid kit in his hand. "Nobody's going to sue you. It's just a minor wound."

While Lindsay thanked Mr. Prior for wiping Garth's arm clean of blood and dressing his scratch with antiseptic and Band-aids, Garth wandered back to the hedge. Lindsay turned around to see him digging a hole in the bare dirt there with a stick he had found.

"Now you stop that, little boy. No digging up my courtyard. I won't have it, hear?" the landlady squawked. She sounded like a flustered parrot.

"I'm sorry," Lindsay said. She lassoed her brother with her arms and began hauling him toward the lobby.

The landlady continued scolding. "Children nowadays have no respect for other people's property. You can't play in this courtyard unless you're going to treat it properly."

"I'm sorry," Lindsay said again from the doorway. Garth was still holding the stick. She tried to pry it out of his fingers, but he wouldn't let go.

"My stick," he said determinedly.

"Of course, Betty," Mr. Prior said, "if you aren't nice to these children, their parents *could* sue you as the owner of the cat that clawed the boy."

Betty turned on him furiously. "And why didn't you catch my cat when you saw it, Stuart? You know how upset I've been since it ran away."

"I'm afraid you flatter me, my dear. Cat catching requires more youth and agility than I have left in me."

Lindsay didn't know what to make of Mr. Prior. He had hidden the cat, so he was a liar. But considering his reason for lying, she couldn't hold it against him.

"Do you like cats, girl?" Betty called to her.

"I like all animals," Lindsay said.

"Well, I'll give you a reward if you can catch my sister's cat and bring it to me. Mr. Prior will tell you where my house is. It's just a few blocks from here."

"No doubt the cat will return to you on its own," Mr. Prior said. "Cats usually return to a good home." The old man winked at Lindsay behind Betty's back.

"It was my dear sister's last request that I care for Sapphire," Betty said. Tears filled her eyes.

"Even though you hate cats," Mr. Prior said.

"Nevertheless, I loved my sister, and I mean to honor her request." Betty fumbled in her purse, but it was Mr. Prior who whipped out a clean white square of handkerchief from his jacket pocket for her to use. "Thank you, Stuart," she sighed. "You do try, don't you?"

"For you? Always," he said.

"I can't understand why no one in this house can trap it for me," the landlady said. "It just comes here because this was where it lived with Sister before she moved in with me. Well . . ." Betty touched her eyes with the handkerchief and cocked her head coyly at the old man. "I came to ask you to go to the museum with me today, Stuart. There's a lecture on that artist you admire—Dürer? It's free."

"It's kind of you to invite me," Mr. Prior said courteously, "but I'm afraid I need to push forward on illustrations my publisher is impatiently awaiting. Perhaps another time."

She raised her eyebrows as if to say it made no difference to her whether he went or not. Then she turned to Lindsay. "You see to it your brother behaves, now," she said, before trotting off on her high heels through the gate.

Silently Mr. Prior pocketed the handkerchief Betty had returned to him. "She is not especially fond of either cats or children," he said. "But otherwise she's not a bad person." He was watching Garth, who had gone back to the hedge. Now he was sticking the bits of yew he'd broken off into the earth where he'd scraped pencil-deep ditches. "You won't turn the cat in, will you, Lindsay?" Mr. Prior asked.

"Oh, no," Lindsay said.

"I thought not." He smiled approvingly at her, nodding to himself. "You have a good day," he said, and he limped back into the lobby.

The sunlight was shining prettily off the ivy in the courtyard which was aglow with morning light. Still, Lindsay felt very alone there. Maybe she should call Rona and tell her about the cat—if Rona was home, if she wasn't over at Jill's. Better to wait until tonight when the long-distance rates would be cheaper.

"Come, Garth." Lindsay took his grubby hand in hers. "Come inside and I'll give you a cookie."

"Kitty gone?" Garth asked. His sky-blue eyes were as innocent as the cat's, but his deformed mouth tore at her like an accusation.

It was her fault they had to be here in Schenectady, her fault Dad needed a better-paying job. He had told her he was giving up making boats because he wanted a different kind of work. After he got trained, he'd said, Mama might even be able to stay home again, the way she had since Garth was born.

20

But Lindsay knew. She knew what they needed the money for and why they'd moved to the city. It was to be near the hospital where Garth would start getting his face fixed. At least three expensive operations, the doctors had said. It might take years. And whose fault was that? Not that her mother or father would ever accuse her. "An accident," they'd said. "It's not your fault, Lindsay." But she knew better.

chapter

3

Garth finally fell asleep about the time Mama was due home. Lindsay draped herself over the living room windowsill to wait for her mother, glad for the chance to rest. She had played inside with Garth most of the day to keep him from tearing up the landlady's precious courtyard. She'd piled up the chairs and cushions for him to climb over, played hide and seek, given him half a roll of paper towels to crayon, and put everything plastic she could find in the bathtub for him to float and fill and sink. She'd read to him and sung to him and let him climb on her back and ride her around the living room. She didn't know how she could keep this up tomorrow and every weekday until school began.

The courtyard was empty and deep in shadow this late in the day, too somber to be inviting. Lindsay wondered if Anna and Amesley had come back. They were too old to be her friends, of course, but Amesley had been nice to invite her to go to the playground this morning. She hoped he'd ask her again some weekend when her parents were home watching Garth and she was free to play. The twins had acted funny about the cat. They seemed to be in a conspiracy with Mr. Prior to hide it from the landlady, even though it belonged to her. That landlady certainly had been nasty about Garth. What harm could he do digging, when the tree was the only pretty thing in the courtyard and he couldn't hurt that?

Because Lindsay's eyes were on the gnarled trunk of the big tree, she spotted the triangular face of the landlady's Siamese cat between the leaves on the lowest branch. The cat was watching Lindsay intently.

"Here, kitty. Here, kitty," Lindsay called. It hadn't touched the bowl of milk she'd put out for it earlier near her own window. She pursed her lips and made a kissy sound. The cat watched her with a black seed of suspicion at the center of its eyes. It was a female, Lindsay decided, because it was too delicate and pretty to be a male.

When the cat stood, she arched her back and then stretched out longer than seemed possible on the limb. She was a coffee-and-cream-colored cat, black coffee on all her tips, coffee streaked with milk on her back and pure cream underneath. She

23

was so beautiful that Lindsay yearned to touch her.

A pale-faced man with unfocused eyes stalked through the gate. His black hair was tied back and hung like a limp snake behind him. ". . . Told that dumb jerk, told him she was no good," the man said as loudly as if he were talking to someone, "but he wouldn't listen to me, never listened, never did one thing I told him. Should have listened to me. Smarmy woman, sucked up to me. Drove that big gas guzzler like she was some kind of big shot . . ." A white carton of take-out food dangled from the tips of the man's fingers by its little metal handle. He stopped under the tree and looked up. "You there, Raki? Well, come on then."

Abruptly he strode on toward the door to the lobby. The cat leaped from the tree and streaked after him. The man held the door open for her. Daintily she stepped in ahead of him.

Now what was all that about, Lindsay wondered. Did that man live here, too? He was weird the way he talked to himself, and even the way he looked— Lindsay hoped he wasn't crazy. It disconcerted her to live in a place where she didn't know people or how anything fit. Tomorrow, if Mr. Prior came into the courtyard, Lindsay would take Garth out there and try to get the old man to tell her who was who around here.

The gate opened again. It wasn't Mama, but Amesley and Anna lugging loaded supermarket bags. Between them, cradling a double armload of books, was a chesty woman in jeans with a face as warm and open as Amesley's.

"So did your teacher like your term paper, Ma?" Anna asked her.

"He hasn't read it yet, honey."

"Why not? You gave it to him two weeks ago," Anna said.

"He still hasn't read it. When he does, he'll give me a good mark. He'll have to because it's a good paper."

"I don't know." A warning note sounded in Anna's voice as if she were the parent. "You handed it in late, Ma. Our teacher last year always marked us down for being late."

"This teacher does that to me, and I'll give him what for!" The woman laughed as she and her daughter passed into the building.

Amesley must have noticed Lindsay in the window because he had stopped short. He was holding a couple of bulging plastic bags in each hand and grinning at her. "How'd you get rid of your brother?"

"He's sleeping."

"Sleeping? That kid didn't look like he'd ever wear out. . . . You never did say what happened to his face."

She flinched as the flashback came at her again. Before it could hit her, she closed herself off. Tonelessly she set out words for Amesley. "He got hit by a horseshoe."

"Ooo!" Amesley winced as if he could feel it.

"Right in the mouth, huh? That's too bad. How did he—"

"Did you have fun at the playground?" She rushed her question at him to fend off his.

"Hit two home runs and started in leathercraft," he said. "You got to have money to do leathercraft. You know, to buy the materials? Last summer I didn't have enough, but this year I earned some, hauling ladies' bundles upstairs and collecting deposit cans."

"I earned money from digging fishing worms when we lived in Schuylerville."

"Yeah? Worms, huh? You fish?"

"A little. Mostly my dad and his friends do."

"Yeah, fishing's okay. Kind of slow, though. So how do you like it here so far?"

"I don't know." She was wary of admitting she hated it. It was his home, after all. "Are you and Anna really twins?"

"Well, we're both thirteen, but Anna's five minutes older so she makes out like she's my big sister every chance she gets. You're what, ten or eleven?"

"Almost twelve. That is, I will be in less than two weeks."

"No kidding! You going to invite me to your birthday party? Don't forget to invite me if you got anything to eat. I love parties and eating—especially eating."

She reflected his floodlight smile without answering. Her birthday would be celebrated back in Schuylerville with Rona and Jill. Mom had promised to take them to the miniature golf course and out for lunch.

"That cat came out of the tree for a man—" Lindsay began.

"A guy with a scraggly ponytail?" Linday nodded. "Yeah, that's Hogan," Amesley said. "He works at the car wash. Goes around talking to himself all the time."

"Is he crazy?"

Amesley shrugged. "Probably. You got to be crazy to live around here, crazy or poor or both."

"But the landlady said she lives near here."

"Yeah, in a street where rich people lived before they tore down most of the big old houses. Betty's got a three-story-high house. And a whole park to herself with an iron fence around it to keep everybody out."

"She lives there alone?"

"Well, she had a husband, but he passed on. And then she had a sister move in with her who just passed on a few weeks ago. No kids."

"She isn't really going to hurt the cat if she catches it, is she?" Lindsay asked.

"Oh, yeah, she'll get it declawed and defanged. She will." Amesley nodded his head seriously. "Betty's a witch. One day late with the rent and she'll evict you."

"She doesn't like my little brother," Lindsay said.

"You better watch out she don't declaw him, too. Best thing would be to take him to the playground. He can mess around all he wants there."

Instead of explaining again that she couldn't, Lindsay asked, "What's the cat's name?"

"Depends on who you're asking. Anna calls her Toasty. Betty's sister called her Sapphire. Hogan calls her Raki—don't ask me why."

The window over Lindsay's head opened and Anna stuck her head out. "Amesley, Mama wants you to bring that stuff up *now*."

"Coming," he said without budging. The courtyard was so deep in shade that night seemed to have fallen even though the sky overhead was still day-blue. Where was Mama, Lindsay wondered just as her mother came through the gate.

"There you are," Lindsay said happily.

"Hi," Mama said. "Where's Garth?"

"He's sleeping. This is Amesley, Mama. He lives upstairs."

"Hello, Amesley." Mama shifted the bag of food she was carrying to her other arm and held out her hand. "I'm Mrs. Carson."

Amesley put down two of his bags so he could reach his hand out to shake. Then he winked at Lindsay over his shoulder and turned back to say to her mother, "Mrs. Carson, you wouldn't mind if Lindsay took her brother to a playground near here, would you? It's got a big sandbox the little guy could dig in and kids his age he could play with."

"The one past the school and across the avenue?" Mama sounded alarmed, and when Amesley nodded she said, "It's too far. And—it's just too far."

⚜

While Mama was heating the dinner, she asked Lindsay how Garth had behaved.

"He was okay," Lindsay said cautiously. "But I wish he had some dirt to play in. The landlady said he can't dig in the courtyard. She was really mad about it, and all he did was scratch around a little."

"I'm sorry, but I don't like the element that hangs out at that playground," Mama said. "I don't want you taking Garth there."

Lindsay sighed. She wondered if she should admit that Garth didn't listen to her the way he used to. Mama didn't see it because he still listened to his parents. It was just Lindsay he kept testing. But admitting she could no longer handle Garth would give Mama more to worry about. It wasn't as if they could afford to hire somebody to take care of him. No, the one thing Lindsay could do to help her parents now was to watch Garth while they worked.

"Maybe you could ask the landlady if she'd let Garth dig if I fill in the holes?" Lindsay said.

"We'll see." Mama sounded vague, which meant she wouldn't do it. She was too shy to ask people for favors, Lindsay knew. Maybe Dad could ask for her. If not, she could try hiding the holes Garth dug and hope she didn't get caught. That was the kind of thing Jill always got away with. She used to sneak around the house of a boy she liked and peek in his windows. And she'd lie to the teacher about why she was late.

Rona did stuff, too, like trespassing when she wanted to take a shortcut. "What are they going to do to me? Shoot me?" she'd said once. Lindsay was the only one who wouldn't do anything wrong—which hadn't saved her from disaster, she thought bitterly.

Garth woke up and came to the kitchen table as soon as he smelled the fried chicken heating. Later, when Dad came home, filling the small apartment with his energetic presence, Lindsay relaxed. Dad got his weights out and pumped his arm muscles while he told them about the manuals he'd been given to study and how trying to figure out all the diagrams and new words made his brain sizzle. "It's like building up a muscle," he said. "You just got to keep working at it and not give up. This guy said he'd put in extra hours with me if I need it."

"Looks like you're going to be working 'round the clock, Bud. You sure you want to do this computer stuff?" Mama asked.

"Sure I'll do it. And you know why?" Dad's broad,

ruddy face bent close to Mom's thin, shadowy one as he answered his own question. "Because I've got a family worth frying my brain for." He kissed Mama, and she folded her arms around his neck and let him sway her back and forth. When they got like that, so intent on each other, they seemed to forget they had children, Lindsay thought. She watched, wondering if she would ever be paired that happily.

"Me, me!" Garth cried. He threw his arms around his parents' legs. Then Dad held an arm out for Lindsay to join in the hug.

Rona called while Mama was putting Garth to bed. "So if you're not mad at me, why wouldn't you talk to me, Lindsay?"

"I don't know, Rona."

"Well, I don't understand what's got into you. You know, Lindsay, you started acting funny even before the move. You're not still shook up about Garth's accident, are you?"

"Of course not," Lindsay said. And to show how normal she was, she said, "There's a cat here. People are trying to hide her from the landlady."

"Oh, right. I know. Most apartments have no pets allowed. And you're in an apartment, not a house, right?"

"Right," Lindsay said. It was too complicated to explain any more about the cat.

"Well, so how are you doing?"

"Okay—so far."

"And what about Garth? How's the little terror?"

"He hasn't done anything awful yet, Rona."

"I think your parents are mean to make you take care of him and not even pay you for it."

"No," Lindsay said. "I want to help. I really do."

"Yeah, well, you better not let him have his way all the time. You've been letting him get away with murder lately, you know."

"No, I haven't."

"Oh? Remember when he was in the hospital, and he wanted your kitten shirt that I gave you, and you took it off and went home in just your jacket?"

"He was in the hospital, Rona."

Rona sighed. "Anyway, I miss you. Jill's always after me to do something and she never shuts up. I don't think that kid ever relaxes her jaw."

Lindsay laughed. "You said she was fun."

"Well, she is. But I like being with you better."

The relief of hearing that was so great it took Lindsay's breath away and she couldn't say another word.

Garth began tugging at her leg and begging her to read him a story. "I have to go," Lindsay told Rona. "'Bye now," and she hung up.

"What do you want me to read you?" she asked Garth.

"Horton."

Dr. Seuss books were his favorites. They had been hers, too. While she held him in her lap with her chin resting on his soft curls and heard her own voice saying aloud the familiar rhymes, she thought about her friendship with Rona. It had taken Lindsay so long to get a friend. She hadn't had any in their country neighborhood when she was little, and she hadn't made any in kindergarten. Dad had laughed at her when he'd asked what she liked about kindergarten and instead of friends, she'd mentioned the big sheets of paper and the story times and the wonderful wooden log construction to climb on in the playground.

In first grade, it had been her agility scampering over and swinging from that log construction that had won Rona's admiration. What a miracle it had been finally to have someone to chase through the fields and share secrets with in the tree house Dad had built! Doing things alone could be fun, but it turned out to be twice as much fun doing them with a friend. And Rona's laugh was big, as big as Rona was.

Rona had been the one who opened their circle to Jill. She'd been the one most taken with Jill's horse and the fish pond. What if Lindsay didn't move back to Schuylerville for a long time, years maybe? Would Rona still prefer her to Jill then?

chapter

4

Two sky-blue eyes were staring right into Lindsay's when she opened them the next morning. "Hi, Garth. You up already?" she asked.

He kissed her. Sometimes he woke up feeling affectionate and liked to cuddle. She'd relished the cuddling before the accident, but now when he pressed his scarred mouth against hers, she felt sick. The bumpy, twisted lips didn't disgust her; they accused her. She had done this to him, and the deed was like a black hole that threatened to suck her in and destroy her. She couldn't talk about it, certainly not to her parents, who had had to change their lives because of Garth's needs. She couldn't even think about it without feeling awful because there was no way to make amends. He had been damaged and she was forever guilty. Choking on her grief, she hugged him.

"I love you, Garth," she whispered in his ear. For an answer he nuzzled her cheek with his cold nose.

"Come on," she said. "Let's go see what's for breakfast." It was only when she moved her legs, knocking his blocks and plastic toys onto the floor, that she realized he'd been playing for a while right on her bed.

"Looks like you two woke up early," Mama said from the doorway. "If you hurry, I'll make you French toast before I go to work."

"Garth's the one who's been up, not me," Lindsay said.

Mama smiled, eyeing the plastic toy train still climbing Lindsay's sheet-covered hip. "You always were a good sleeper, Lindsay. . . . You help your sister pick up now, Garth. Hear?"

The minute Mama left, Garth rolled under her bed to watch while Lindsay put his toys back in the box without even trying to make him help.

"I was thinking, Lindsay," Mama said as she served them the cinnamon-sweet toast. "Your father's working Saturday and I've got errands to do, but what if I drop you and Garth off at the playground and pick you up there? On Saturdays parents should be around to keep an eye on things."

"Sure, Mama." But that left four days to get through until the weekend, Lindsay thought. What was she going to do with Garth? Maybe if she took some of his trucks outside, he'd be willing to play with them and not dig. Morning sunshine beckoned her from the courtyard. Yes, she told herself, that might work.

"I'll bring you a Tootsie Pop this evening, Garth," Mama promised him before she left. "But you only get it if Lindsay tells me you were a good boy for her today. Understand?"

"I'm good," Garth assured her. His faith in his own goodness was unshakable, no matter what mischief he had done. Mama tousled his hair, gave each of them a quick kiss good-bye, and left for work. From the back she looked like a boy, walking off in her uniform. Only the brown hair curling over her shoulders was girlish.

Life had been such fun when Garth was born and Mama quit her rural delivery route to stay home, Lindsay recalled. Together Mama and she had bathed and diapered the chubby baby, kissed his toes, and made him laugh. And sometimes Mama had driven Lindsay over to Rona's. And sometimes Lindsay had brought Rona home from school with her to play with her baby brother. Then Mama would bake molasses cookies for them. But that had been before the accident. Before the accident—that time seemed like a fairy tale now.

Lindsay collected some of Garth's trucks and told him they were going out. Instantly he picked up his shovel. "No, Garth, you can't dig. The lady who owns this building won't let you."

"She gone."

"But she might come."

"Then I hide."

"But she'll know who dug the hole."

"No."

"No, what?" Lindsay asked.

"I dig." He planted his feet apart, made fists, and narrowed his eyes. Next he'd start wailing and keep it up until Lindsay felt crazy enough to scream herself.

"Garth, please," she begged. "You'll get us both in trouble."

"No."

"Then we can't go outside." Frustrated, she went to lean on the windowsill.

Mr. Prior was sitting on his bench in the shade reading a newspaper. Sapphire leaped lightly into his lap. Mr. Prior spoke to the cat and readjusted the newspaper to accommodate her. Now would be the time to make friends with Sapphire, while the cat felt secure in the protection of someone she knew. But Lindsay couldn't go outside and leave Garth alone in the apartment.

There was a crash in the kitchen. Lindsay scolded Garth as she picked up the broken plates. Somehow, he'd pulled the drainboard down.

"I didn't do it," he said.

"Yes, you did, Garth. You broke these dishes."

"No. You did."

"You were a bad boy."

"No, you bad." He grinned at her as if it were a game.

She couldn't win by arguing with him because he skipped around reason as if it weren't there. In disgust she gave up and took him out to the courtyard after all.

They walked through the dank lobby, past the mysteriously unmarked doors that led, Dad said, to storage areas or down into the fearful blackness of the furnace room. The tiled floor that had once been white was now shades of black and gray from neglect. It was a relief to step out into the courtyard.

Mr. Prior was snoozing. His newspaper had fallen to the ground and the cat was stretched out along his legs, her head hanging over his knees.

Lindsay set Garth's trucks down and discovered he'd brought out his shovel. Again she explained to him why he couldn't dig. Again he refused to understand.

"Garth, you don't act like a baby with Mama. Why do it with me?" He grinned at her as if they both knew the answer to that. Since the accident she hadn't been able to refuse him anything.

Garth went immediately to a spot of bare earth under the tree and began to dig. If she let him be and the landlady came and yelled at him, would that scare him into behaving himself? Maybe. Maybe not, though. And what if the landlady got angry enough to kick the Carson family out or charge Mama for damages?

Lindsay bit her thumb as she tried to untangle the problem.

"What's wrong, Lindsay?" Mr. Prior asked. He was awake now and stroking the cat, whose body flowed over his legs like molten lava.

"Do you know when the landlady comes by, Mr. Prior?" Lindsay asked.

"It varies," he said. "She visits us when she has time on her hands. Sometimes we don't see her for weeks. But I'm afraid she'll be upset if she catches your little brother digging up her courtyard. You see, this place was elegant when her husband bought it forty-odd years ago, and Betty simply isn't aware of how it's deteriorated." His eyes showed a sad amusement.

"Garth, please stop. Come here. Please!" Lindsay called helplessly. He didn't stop and didn't come. She hadn't expected he would. "Digging's his favorite thing," she explained to Mr. Prior. "I thought maybe if I filled in the holes . . ."

"I'm afraid Betty's no more reasonable than Garth. If she notices, she'll have a fit."

Lindsay crouched and stroked the cat with one finger, trying to think of what she should do.

Sapphire's blue eyes blinked open sleepily and closed again as she decided Lindsay was no threat. Her well-groomed fur felt satiny under Lindsay's fingertips.

"I guess I better keep Garth inside then," Lindsay said. The notion depressed her more than ever.

"Now that would be a shame on such a pretty summer day," Mr. Prior said. "Can't you make him behave?" Lindsay shook her head.

Mr. Prior persisted gently, "You'd stop him if he were doing something dangerous, wouldn't you?"

"Yes." She saw what he meant. "Well, like if he's playing with matches or something, I can drag him away. But he bites and kicks and he'll yell and yell and just keep yelling. He can yell forever."

"I'm surprised that your mother leaves him with you if he's that difficult."

"He's not a bad boy, Mr. Prior. And he used to listen to me. Mama thinks he still does, I guess. He's pretty good when she and Dad are around."

Mr. Prior's hooded eyes gleamed with sympathy as he studied her, his head nodding thoughtfully. "Why is that?" he asked. "That you used to be able to control him and now you can't?"

Lindsay shrugged, unwilling to answer. Instead she asked, "Do you really think the landlady would hurt the cat if you let her catch it?"

"That depends on what you consider hurtful.

She's likely to have it declawed because her house is full of valuable antiques which she's anxious to preserve. And she may have its teeth filed because she's afraid of animals. Also, she will probably confine it to an empty upstairs room where she will conscientiously feed it and change its litter box—but that's likely to be the extent of her care for her sister's pet."

Lindsay shuddered.

"Exactly. It would be a pity to cripple this beautiful creature and keep her in solitary confinement." Mr. Prior's papery-skinned hand was stroking the fur under the cat's lifted chin now. "The problem is, Betty doesn't believe that cats have feelings," Mr. Prior said. "Of course, we know they do, don't we?"

"And she won't listen to you?"

He chuckled. "No more than your little brother listens to you." Mischief gleamed under his heavy eyelids. "I'll tell you what, though," he said. "If we can hide this cat from Betty, it's likely we can hide a few holes. You don't think he plans to dig up the whole yard, do you?"

They both looked doubtfully at Garth, who had already made a pail-sized hole. "What we need," Mr. Prior said, "is a lid we can throw on in a hurry. Something like a piece of plywood."

"But won't Betty notice that?"

"I'll tell her the no-good janitor she hired left it there. The fellow rarely shows up before payday."

Mr. Prior laughed, a wheezy laugh that came from high in his chest.

"What's so funny?" Anna wanted to know. She had come out of the house and was standing behind Lindsay.

"Just a private joke," Mr. Prior said. "And what are you up to on this beautiful morning, Anna?"

"I'm going to the library. I read to little kids there Tuesdays."

"That sounds like fun."

"Last week I read them one of your books, Mr. Prior," Anna said.

"Did you? And did they enjoy it?" Mr. Prior asked.

"Well—" Anna's long face was serious as she considered the question. "They fidgeted, but it was short and I read fast."

Mr. Prior winced.

Quickly Lindsay said, "I never knew anyone who was a writer before. What kind of books do you write?"

"Little ones for little children. Mostly I'm an illustrator, actually," Mr. Prior said. "Mostly I *was* an illustrator, I should say. Publishers don't seem eager to pay for my efforts lately." His smile was pained.

"There's a whole shelf of books in the library with Mr. Prior's name on them," Anna said. "He draws little animals a lot."

"Can you walk to the library from here?" Lindsay asked Anna.

"Oh, sure. Come on and I'll show you. You can get a card real easy."

"No, thanks," Lindsay said regretfully. "I've got to watch Garth."

"Brothers are such a pain," Anna said. Her eyes were on Garth, who was rapidly extending the sides of his hole outward. "Amesley got in trouble again and Mama has him washing all the walls in the apartment for punishment. So now *I* can't go to the playground today."

"She won't let you go alone?" Lindsay asked.

"She doesn't like us to go anywhere alone, except to the library."

"May I ask what kind of trouble our amiable Amesley got into?" Mr. Prior sounded genuinely curious.

"Oh, him!" Anna said with disgust. "This kid that Amesley plays ball with asked him to hide a shoebox full of stolen stuff for him. See, the kid's guardian was onto him and was looking. So Amesley agreed. You'd think he'd know better. I mean he didn't even ask the kid what was in the box. And Mama noticed it under his bed. She notices everything." Anna's eyes sparked with the energy of her telling. "Mama really gave it to Amesley. She says she's going to march him down to the jail and show him what it's like inside because that's where he's headed. Not that Amesley's bad," Anna said quickly. "Just stupid."

"Amesley will no doubt be grateful for your mother's vigilance someday," Mr. Prior said.

Anna raised a doubtful eyebrow and stroked the cat, who rolled into a ball to keep from being bothered. "Toasty, you scamp," Anna said. "I know why you're pooped this morning. You were catching mice all night, weren't you? And you left one right at the top of my stairs."

"She was giving you a present," Mr. Prior said. "Cats'll do that."

"Amesley let her in our apartment, and she was sleeping on my bed again last night," Anna said. "But then Ma must have put her out when she got back from school."

"Your mother goes to school at night?" Lindsay said. "So does my dad sometimes."

"Ma's getting her teaching degree," Anna said proudly. "Right now she's just an aide, but when she gets her degree, she'll be a regular teacher."

"And you'll follow in her footsteps, I suspect," Mr. Prior said.

"Teach bratty little kids? Not me," Anna said. "I'm going to be a Supreme Court judge."

Mr. Prior and Lindsay stared at her openmouthed.

"Well," Anna said, "why not?"

"Why not indeed!" Mr. Prior said.

"I gotta go," Anna said. "See you all later." She

walked off regally, but at the gate she turned and advised Garth, "You're going to be in *big* trouble digging that hole, kid. The witch'll screech your ears out when she sees it."

Garth looked up at her wide-eyed and stopped digging. "But if she's mean to you, you'll probably deserve it," Anna concluded before she turned and passed through the gate.

"She might end up a judge at that," Mr. Prior said.

Sapphire stood, arched her back, and yawned. Then she jumped lightly from Mr. Prior's lap and rubbed herself against Lindsay's legs. Delighted, Lindsay reached to pick her up, but Sapphire slipped through her fingers.

"Her Majesty gives her affection only when she chooses," Mr. Prior said. At the base of the tree Sapphire stretched up to rake the bark with her front claws.

Garth stopped digging and came to Lindsay. "Juice," he demanded.

"Sure," she said. "Come inside."

"No. You get it for me, Lindsay."

"Would it be all right if I left him here with you for a minute, Mr. Prior?" she asked.

"If it's not a long enough minute for him to get in trouble. Better fill in that hole when you come back, or cover it with something."

Lindsay brought Garth a glass of juice and one for Mr. Prior as well. She planned to drink it herself if he didn't want it, but he accepted it with obvious pleasure. "Thank you, dear child," he said.

She quickly filled in the hole Garth had dug. Luckily, he didn't notice. He had settled down to playing with his trucks in a shadier section of the courtyard.

"He's got you well trained, hasn't he?" Mr. Prior said.

Lindsay gave him a polite smile, although she knew his question was a criticism.

"Did he stop listening to you after whatever happened to his face?" Mr. Prior asked gently.

"He got hit by a horseshoe," Lindsay said breathlessly. "I didn't throw it." She edged toward the apartment house to avoid any further questions. "Garth, we have to go in now," she called. Her brother ignored her.

Lindsay glanced at Mr. Prior and flushed, but he said only, "I suppose I had best get to my drafting table and do some work, whether anyone wants it or not. That's what I do with my life, after all. See you later, Lindsay." He limped off toward the lobby.

A pale yellow butterfly cruised the ivy and fluttered away. Lindsay yearned for the fields full of butterflies and Queen Anne's lace in Schuylerville. Last summer, she and Rona had made wildflower arrangements to sell for a quarter at the roadside. Rona liked doing things that earned money. She had offered to sell Lindsay's bears for her.

Lindsay's eyes sought Garth. Where was he? His trucks were abandoned by the washtub-sized hole she'd just filled in. "Garth!" Lindsay yelled. Through the open gate, she saw a flash of curly blond hair. He was outside on the sidewalk!

"Better catch him before he runs into the street," Mr. Prior said from the door to the lobby.

Expecting any second to hear the screech of brakes, Lindsay dashed after her brother.

chapter

5

"Garth!" Lindsay screamed out in the street, but nobody was there to hear her. The sidewalk was empty in both directions. She checked behind the bulky bags of garbage overflowing the cans at the curb. No Garth. Two delivery trucks and a car were waiting for the light to change at the intersection. Desperately she searched for a curly golden head.

Across the street, next to a fence scrawled with graffiti, the marquee of an old movie theater advertised films for adults only. A teenage boy with a weird haircut and cutoff T-shirt bopped by with unseeing eyes. Where had Garth disappeared to so fast? Down this side of the street was a grocery store. A sign in the window said *Aquí se habla español*, but the sign on the door was turned to *Closed*. Up the street was a narrow, dingy apartment building with an entrance a step above the sidewalk. Had he run in there?

Her heart gyrated so wildly she felt nauseous. It was like the time she'd been in charge of Garth at the picnic. She'd done it again. How could she have done it again?

Her legs trembled as she ran to check out the narrow building. Its entrance door was locked. Farther up the street were storefronts advertising vacuum cleaner repairs, a photography studio, and The Economy Mart. As Lindsay hesitated about which to try, she saw Amesley coming out of The Economy Mart carrying a new mop in one hand. The other hand held Garth's. They strolled toward her through a sprawl of furnishings outside a used furniture store—armchair, umbrella stand, a stack of tables, part of a kitchen set.

"Garth, why did you run away?" Lindsay shouted at him.

He acted as if he didn't know her.

"I was buying this mop," Amesley said, "and I see this little guy nosing around the shop like his pocket's full of money."

"Why did you run out of the courtyard, Garth?" Lindsay asked again. "That was bad, bad. You scared me half to death."

Garth smiled as if that were an achievement.

"Listen, kid." Amesley squatted so he was nose to nose with Garth. "You want to do what your big sister says or you could get hurt. People in this neighborhood going to squash you like a cockroach just for the fun of it. You too short to go out alone. Get it?"

"Hi, guy," Garth said. He patted Amesley's cheek.

Amesley threw back his head and chortled. "You got to admit the kid's got style," he said.

"It won't help Lindsay to make her brother think he's funny, Amesley," Mr. Prior said. He was standing at the gate to their apartment house, leaning on his cane.

Garth gazed adoringly up at Amesley, who led him back into the courtyard followed by Mr. Prior and Lindsay.

"How will you convince him not to run off like that again?" Mr. Prior asked Lindsay.

"I could tell my mother when she gets home tonight," she said without enthusiasm. "Or I could just keep him indoors. . . . Maybe that's what I better do."

They all looked at Garth who had reclaimed his shovel and was beginning to turn over the soft dirt of the filled-in hole. "You're punishing yourself for his naughtiness if you keep him inside," Mr. Prior said.

"What would you do, Mr. Prior?" Amesley asked with interest.

"Get a rope and tie him to the tree." Mr. Prior

spoke so solemnly that Lindsay couldn't tell if he was joking or not.

"Yeah, right. Good idea," Amesley said, widening his eyes while his mouth suppressed a smile.

Lindsay squirmed. She didn't see anything funny about it. "He's only run away once," she said. "And he'd scream bloody murder if I tied him up."

Mr. Prior nodded. "Undoubtedly," he said. "But what if he does?"

"Garth," she said. "Are you going to be a good boy and stay in the courtyard from now on?"

"Uh-huh." He gave her a confident grin.

"Not much of a talker, is he?" Mr. Prior said. His smooth turtle face watched Garth as if he didn't much like the little boy.

In her brother's defense, Lindsay said, "Back in Schuylerville, Garth had lots of space to dig in, plus a swing and climbing bars." She choked up thinking of home. "It's too cramped for him here."

Mr. Prior surveyed the courtyard as if seeing it afresh. "It is small," he said. "It is a very small corner of the world." He nodded to himself, adding, "Amazing that I've spent half a century in this spot."

"Well, but the tree is nice," Lindsay hastened to say in case she'd made him feel bad.

"Kitty," Garth said. The cat was now rolling sensuously in the soft dirt of the hole Lindsay had filled. Her paws flopped above her cream-colored belly. Garth threw himself on her, and she cried out in alarm, squeezed out of his grasp, and escaped through the hedge. No way could she make friends with Sapphire while Garth was around, Lindsay thought.

"I got some walls to scrub and then I'm going to the playground," Amesley said to Lindsay. "Want me to take the little squirt?"

"No, thanks. My mother says she'll take us Saturday."

"*Saturday?* You're going to hang out here till then?" Amesley's cheek and eyebrow went up in doubt. "Well, okay. See you later. 'Bye, squirt." He faked a punch at Garth and sauntered into the house.

"Lindsay," Mr. Prior said as he studied Garth. "That little cherub has the makings of an imp. You'd best start disciplining him for his own good."

Lindsay bit her lip in silence. Mr. Prior didn't understand. She couldn't deny Garth anything, not after what she'd done to him.

At the door to the house, Mr. Prior turned. "At least you'll tell your parents that he ran off, won't you?"

"I don't know," she murmured.

"You don't like to tell on him, I'm sure, but what if he runs out in the street again?" Mr. Prior argued. "Isn't it better to set him up for a thorough scolding than risk his getting hurt?"

He waited while she struggled with his advice. Finally he said, "You think about it. I know you've got your brother's best interests at heart."

And immediately Lindsay asked herself, did she? Did she really love Garth as much as she thought she did, or was she secretly jealous of him and glad to see him hurt? Probably she had resented it at the picnic when her parents stuck her with her little brother. They had taken advantage of her. Dad had, anyway, because she was the good girl, Mama's right hand. So she had held on to Garth instead of joining in the softball game with her friends. That was how it had been, hadn't it? And then she had taken Garth to the place where the men were pitching horseshoes so she wouldn't have to watch her friends having fun without her. Yes, that was how it must have been.

The cat stood at her feet. "Mew?" it asked. Sorrowfully, Lindsay bent and stroked the small, elegant head. The cat's hard skull pushed against her fingers, somehow easing Lindsay's ache.

"Kitty," Garth said.

"You have to be very, very gentle or the kitty will run away, Garth," she told him. Obeying her for once, he crouched and poked the cat with the tip of one pudgy finger. Sapphire rubbed against Lindsay's bare legs in a silken caress.

"She likes us, Garth. See how she likes us?"

"Pretty kitty," Garth observed.

"Oh, she's beautiful. Sapphire's the right name for her."

Garth made a grab for the long, brown wand of a tail.

Sapphire jumped and landed on one of the plastic bags filled with leaves under their apartment window. There she sat whipping her tail angrily back and forth. Now black moons eclipsed the blue of her eyes.

Lindsay sighed. "She hates having her tail pulled, Garth. You made her mad. Come on, I'll give you peanut butter crackers for lunch."

He tucked his hand in hers and let her lead him inside.

Later on, Lindsay got Garth out of the bath that had occupied him for an hour of happy splashing. She wiped up the bathroom floor and took him to the courtyard window, where they leaned side by side on the sill to wait for Mama to come home.

"Mama bring me Tootsie Pop," Garth said.

"No. You were bad today, Garth. You ran into the street, remember?"

"No, I didn't." His mouth drooped and his gaze reproached her.

"Yes, you did." His lower lip folded out. Next he would cry. "Oh, all right, just don't do it again, and I won't tell Mama," Lindsay said.

Hogan came loping through the entryway, swinging the metal handle of his cardboard dinner box from the tips of his fingers the way he had the night before. Lindsay wondered if he ate the same thing every night. The cat backed down the tree trunk, rump wobbling ridiculously in her hurry.

". . . Got his fancy car, got his cellular phone, got his silk socks and shined-up shoes," Hogan muttered. "Stupid chickenhead gonna sue. Not my fault. Not my fault the stupid car gets caught. Take it out of my salary and I'll kill them." He backhanded the tree trunk with his bare hand and the cat, who had been right at his heels, jumped and waited with arched back before continuing to follow Hogan into the house.

Lindsay wondered if he had hurt his hand, smacking it against the rough bark of the tree like that. He was such a scary man. She hoped she never met him alone in the dark lobby.

The landlady was the next through the gate. She minced along in heels so high that Lindsay expected her to tilt and fall any second. On her flowered silk dress she wore a long rope of pearls, and her hair made a tarnished halo around her seamed face. Her eyes picked out Lindsay in the window. "Well, have you found my cat yet, girl?"

"No," Lindsay said.

"But you've seen it about, haven't you?"

Lindsay envied Mr. Prior's easy lying. Lies stuck in her throat, unless they were white lies, like saying somebody looked nice when they didn't. "Your cat's hard to catch," Lindsay said.

"Offer her something to eat, girl. That'll get her."

"Excuse me," Lindsay said. She shut the window and took Garth into the bathroom.

"I don't have to go," he said.

"We're hiding," she whispered.

"Oh." He buried his face in her jeans as if that hid him even more. She stroked his hair. It was softer than the cat's fur.

"Lindsay, where are you?"

"Here, Mama." Lindsay opened the bathroom door. There was Mama unloading a box of pizza at the card table. "Dad's working again tonight?" Lindsay guessed.

The dark half-moons under Mama's eyes lifted with her smile. "You got it. You have a good day?"

"Fine," Lindsay said. Another lie when it would have been such a relief to tell the truth.

"Fine," Garth echoed.

"I guess mine was fine, too, then." Mama gave them each a hug. On the pizza were black olives for Lindsay, pepperoni slices for Garth, and plain cheese and tomato for Mama. Dad, who hated pizza, would probably grab a hamburger for supper somewhere. "Dad's having a hard time being back in school, isn't he, Mama?" Lindsay asked.

"Oh, don't you worry, Lindsay. Your father does

56

what he sets his mind to do. It may be hard for him, but he'll get there."

"Do you hate *your* job, Mama?"

"No, it's okay. I know the forms now. And there was an old lady who came in with a poodle dressed up in a rhinestone collar. Lindsay, would you believe she bought stamps for that dog and pretended he was the one collecting them?" Mama laughed, the way she used to about the foibles of people on her rural delivery route.

"But you said there's no windows where you work," Lindsay reminded her.

"Oh, the day goes by so fast I don't think about looking out." Mama stroked Lindsay's hair back. "You know, you worry too much," she said. Then she gave Garth his Tootsie Pop and told him not to eat it until after supper.

❖

That night, when her parents were watching the news on TV after Garth had gone to sleep, Lindsay called Rona. Rona was the only person she could confide in about Garth.

"He ran out into the street today," she told Rona.

"So lay down the law to him and mean it. You're bigger than he is, Lindsay. Make him behave. You used to, remember?"

"But it's hard for him here. He has no place to play."

"So? Isn't it hard for you, too?" Rona asked.

"He's only a little kid. He doesn't understand."

"What do your parents say?" Rona wanted to know.

"I haven't told them."

"Well, you should."

It was just what Mr. Prior had said and Lindsay didn't want to hear it again. "So what are you doing tomorrow?" she asked.

"Jill's mother's driving us to the lake to swim. What are you doing?"

"Watching Garth."

"Didn't you make any friends there yet?"

"No. There's that cat I told you about, though. It's really cute."

"Lindsay, you know if I could, I'd help you take care of Garth," Rona said. "I wish I could help."

"I know." Rona's good will was comforting. "Don't worry, Rona. I'll make him behave. Tomorrow I won't let him get away with a thing."

"You better not. Listen, your birthday's not so far off, and we'll be together then, right?"

"Right," Lindsay said. She went straight to bed after the phone call because tomorrow she was going to get tough with Garth. And for that she'd need all her strength.

chapter

6

Thunder woke Lindsay. Within seconds rippling sheets of rain were hitting the barred window of her bedroom. She looked at the clock. It was after nine A.M. No wonder Garth's bed was empty, his toys strewn over his rumpled covers. Still wearing the long T-shirt and underpants she'd slept in, Lindsay went looking for her brother.

Mama had left a note on the kitchen table for her. "Told Garth not to wake you up. He promised to be good. Let me know if he's not. I made tuna fish for lunch, with tomato the way you like it. See you tonight, Love, Mama."

The television was on, but Garth wasn't watching it. He wasn't in the kitchen or the bathroom either. How had he gotten out of the apartment? He couldn't open the front door because the doorknob was too hard for him to work.

The living room window was open. Rain was splashing onto the windowsill and onto the scarred and blackened parquet floor beneath it. Would he have gone into the courtyard in this downpour? Lindsay leaned out to look. Garth wasn't outside. Blobby drops of rain splashed up from the concrete steppingstones. Rain washed the ivy's green face and bounced in translucent tears off the bare ground.

Panic-stricken, Lindsay told herself he *must* have gone out the window, the way he had yesterday, out into this fierce shower. Had he run off into the street again? She hurried back to the bedroom for her sandals and took a quick look under both beds just in case he was hiding there. She even thought to check out their parents' bedroom closet before she unlocked the front door. Her fingers fumbled getting the door open, and she left it ajar to race through the musty lobby and outside.

One minute under that power shower soaked Lindsay to the skin. It wasn't warm out this morning, either. She shivered, not from the cold, but from the thought of the terrible things that could be happening to her brother.

"Garth!" she shouted. "Garth!" She stood under the tree, searching its branches. Stupid, she told herself, Garth's not a cat, and he's too young to climb trees yet. She sprinted out of the courtyard into the street.

The grocery with the Spanish sign was the only store open this early. In it, a thickset old man stopped stacking cans of black bean soup to assure her in sweetly accented English that he had not seen a little blond boy. No, not in his store that morning.

She ran a block, two blocks. Her eyes swung from one side of the street to the other as she skated through the rain on fear-swift feet. If Mama had left for work at her usual time, Garth could have been gone for an hour or more. He could have been kidnapped by someone in a passing car. A pervert could be holding him in one of those closed buildings.

Lindsay moaned and pushed back her panic. Why had she slept so long? Why didn't she wake up early the way Garth and Mama did? And why, oh why, had she let her parents go on believing she was capable of taking care of her little brother?

"Garth," she cried helplessly. She saw a car wash sign, remembered Hogan, and dashed across the avenue. A startled man in a pickup truck screeched to a stop to avoid hitting her. The car wash place was closed. Well, it was raining. People didn't need their cars washed in the rain.

She returned the way she'd come and stopped, panting, in front of the courtyard gate, uncertain about which way to go next. Her muscles were knotted up. She bit her lip and tasted blood.

"What happened to you? What are you doing running around in the rain without anything over you?" It was Anna, her long, sensible face framed by the hood of a red plastic raincoat. She was further protected by a huge black umbrella.

"My brother's gone. I can't find him," Lindsay said.

"That kid again? He's some troublemaker. You better whip him into shape before he wrecks your life, girl."

Lindsay began crying. The silent tears blended with the rain.

"Well, come inside and get some dry clothes on before you get pneumonia." Anna said. "Then I'll help you look for him."

The promise of help was comforting, but then Anna asked how Lindsay knew Garth had gone out into the street again. "I don't know anything except he wasn't in the apartment," Lindsay said.

"Could be he's running around the halls nice and dry. Did you think of that?" Anna scolded her. "We'll look for him soon as you get into something dry."

Lindsay was too shaken to object to Anna treating her as if she were a child and Anna an adult. "I don't need to change," Lindsay said. Every second counted when Garth might be in danger. She darted into the lobby.

"Look at that!" Anna sounded shocked. "You left your door wide open."

Lindsay glanced at the door without concern. Garth wasn't in the lobby. Had he gone up the stairs, then? If so, which ones? The stairs on the left led to Hogan's apartment, which was above Mr. Prior's. The ones on the right led to Anna's apartment, which was over Lindsay's.

"Leaving your door open's dangerous," Anna lectured. "Some druggie could come in off the street and rip you off. Or he could wait in there to jump you. You and Hogan! He leaves his door unlocked even though Betty yells at him about it all the time. Are you as crazy as him?"

"Anna, my brother's only three years old," Lindsay cried.

"I know that. Well, you change your clothes while I check the upstairs halls."

Anna set off. Lindsay dashed into her apartment, yanked off her soaked T-shirt, and grabbed a dry one from a drawer, along with a pair of shorts which she pulled on over her sandals and wet underpants. She rechecked the hiding places in the apartment in case Garth had wandered back in, then went to the foot of the stairs and yelled, "Anna?"

"He's not up here." It was Amesley. He was wearing shorts and a white T-shirt that exposed his belly button. "Give me a chance to put on my sneaks and I'll help you look," he said. "Anna went to see if he's at Mr. Prior's."

"Thanks, Amesley," Lindsay said. The more people helping her search, the better. She raced across the lobby just as Mr. Prior stepped out of his apartment with Anna.

"We should try the basement," Mr. Prior was saying. "I'll get a flashlight." A minute later he had joined the search party.

The heavy door to the basement was unlocked and unmarked, but it was unlikely any child, even one as fearless as Garth, would venture into that dungeon-like space that smelled of mold and damp.

"I haven't been down there in years," Mr. Prior said. "But there are storage rooms, and the furnace room of course, and a place where the janitor slept in the days when this building had a full-time janitor."

Lindsay called her brother's name. Silence answered her. She could sense the others' reluctance, so she started down the stairs alone.

"Lindsay," Mr. Prior called. "I doubt anyone's been down in the basement recently. Look." He ran the flashlight beam up and down the steps she was descending.

She understood immediately. So did the others. "No little footprints in the dust," Amesley said. "The kid must've gone out on the street."

"There's one other place we didn't look," Anna said.

"Hogan's apartment," Mr. Prior said. "They close the car wash when it rains, so he may be home."

"Yeah, well, if we're going up to Hogan's, we'd better all go together," Anna said.

"Right," Amesley said. "And you gonna be the one to knock on his door, Anna?"

"I don't know that we need to be so fearful," Mr. Prior said. "Hogan may talk to himself, but he appears harmless."

"You knock then," Anna said. "I went up there one time to sell him raffle tickets for our church, and he blasted open that door so fast it scared me dumb. Then I see him standing there in his underwear with a kitchen knife in his hand. Believe you me, I ran so hard I tripped down the last three steps and broke the heel off my shoe."

"Told you not to wear your Sunday shoes to go collecting in," Amesley said coolly.

Lindsay shuddered. Hogan was probably chopping Garth up into little pieces even as they stood there. "I'll knock," she said. She crossed the lobby to the stairs next to Mr. Prior's apartment and went up them. To her relief the others stayed close behind her.

She rapped timidly on Hogan's door and then more sharply. A television seemed to be playing inside—unless Hogan was talking to someone. And there was a clicking noise. But the loudest sound Lindsay heard was her own heartbeat. When nothing happened, Mr. Prior tapped on the door with his cane.

"Think he doesn't hear us?" Amesley said. He yelled, "Hey, Hogan. Open up. We got to talk to you about something important."

Suddenly there was silence in the apartment. What now? Lindsay screamed her brother's name. The door was flung open. Hogan stood there glowering at them, dressed in his usual workshirt and pants. "What do you want?" he demanded.

Lindsay gave a strangled cry. There was Garth standing naked on a chair, leaning over a small pool table with a cue stick in his hands. "Garth!" She rushed to her brother, followed by the other three. "What happened? Did he hurt you?" She took him into her arms.

"Lemme go," Garth said. "I play pool with Hogan."

"But where are your clothes?"

"Wet," Garth said. "Look, see Kitty?" He pointed toward the only other object in the room, a couch with a sleeping bag spread out on it and the cat stretched like a long fur scarf down the middle. Promptly Garth wriggled out of Lindsay's arms and off the chair. He went to the couch and petted the cat very carefully. "See?" he said when it didn't stir. Triumphantly he grinned over his shoulder at Lindsay.

"He come to the door and I let him in," Hogan said. "I didn't hurt him."

"But where are his clothes?" Mr. Prior asked.

"Drying in the oven. He was wet. He just come. Like the cat."

"Very good of you to take him in, Hogan," Mr. Prior said.

Hogan nodded moodily. "Didn't know whose kid he was," he said. "I was going to take him to the police station when his clothes got dry."

Lindsay retrieved Garth's shorts and T-shirt from the open oven door in the bare, clean kitchen. The clothes were still wet, but warm. A scraggly houseplant was growing on a windowsill that overlooked the alley and the wall of the next building. Briefly she wondered if Hogan had rescued the plant from a garbage bin. Could a crazy man who talked to himself and refused to lock his apartment door be kind? She didn't know. She had no measurement for anyone in this building because she'd never met people like them before.

Hogan stood there in his bare living room, his arms folded across his chest, frowning at his uninvited guests.

"Come on, Garth. Let's go now," Lindsay said after she had gotten him into his clothes.

"No. I play pool."

"You listen to your sister, Garth," Amesley said. "Say 'bye to Mr. Hogan, 'cause we're gone now."

"You play with me?" Garth asked, hopefully inserting his hand into Amesley's.

"Later," Amesley said.

"Tell Mr. Hogan thank you," Lindsay said. She no longer believed that Hogan had molested her brother because Garth seemed so at ease. But she wanted to get out of there because *she* wasn't at ease with Hogan.

"Thanks," Garth obliged her by saying.

"Somebody messed up his mouth," Hogan said, making it a statement rather than a question.

Lindsay tensed. They were all standing there watching her, and suddenly the simple explanation that Garth had been hit by a horseshoe wasn't enough. "It was my fault," she blurted out in anguish. "I was supposed to watch him at the picnic, but I took him to see the men pitching horseshoes, and I let go of him and he—" She swallowed and confessed in a whisper. "He ran right in the path of the shoe." Her eyes closed to shut out the horror, the memory of the hard metal object smashing into her little brother's soft angel face, and the blood and the screams. She kept her eyes closed to avoid their shock at what she'd done.

The room was very quiet for a minute. Then Hogan said, "I got scars." Lindsay opened her eyes. Hogan was unbuttoning his shirt to show them his chest, which was a ropy landscape of burn marks, slick areas of skin between twisting welts.

"Wow!" Amesley said. "That must've hurt plenty."

"I don't remember," Hogan said. "I was just a little kid." He rebuttoned his shirt. Then he bent to the pool table, sliding a cue stick deftly through the crook of his finger and ignoring them.

The balls clicked as Lindsay and the others said their good-byes and clicked again as they shut the door behind them.

"Whew," Anna said when they had arrived back downstairs in the lobby. "That was weird."

"That guy, you think he's got any friends?" Amesley asked Mr. Prior.

"I doubt he has," Mr. Prior said. "He's too lacking in social skills."

"Huh?" Amesley said.

"Unlike you, Amesley," Mr. Prior said.

"I got friends," Garth said.

"And who may they be?" Mr. Prior asked.

"Kitty," Garth said. "I pet him."

"Her," Anna said. "Toasty's a girl."

"Her name's really Sapphire," Lindsay said.

"Hogan, who feeds her, calls her Raki," Mr. Prior said.

"But what about Betty's sister?" Anna asked.

"A dead woman can't own a cat. And Betty shouldn't own one," Mr. Prior said.

Just to make sure, Lindsay asked quietly, "Garth, did Hogan touch you, you know, on your private parts or ask you to touch him on his?"

"Uh-uh," Garth said. "He teached me pool." Lindsay sighed with relief, her last qualm satisfied.

"You worry too much about this kid," Anna said. "You're too little yourself to be his mother. Why don't you just relax and give him a swat when he does something bad?" She bent down, looking like a plastic-coated witch in her red raincoat, and told Garth, "You're bad to run out of the house and scare your sister. You don't stop that and *I'll* swat you one."

Garth took a step back from her and grabbed Lindsay's hand.

"His sister is the one who must discipline him, Anna," Mr. Prior said. "We can't do it for her because we're not with Garth enough."

They all looked at Lindsay, and she knew they were thinking about Garth's face.

"It wasn't your fault," Amesley said. "If you were just holding the kid, and he got loose, it was an accident."

Garth tugged her toward their apartment. "Let's go, Lindsay," he said.

She let him pull at her without moving. "I let him go," she repeated to Amesley, to Mr. Prior, to Anna. "I was supposed to watch him, and I let him go."

"It was still an accident," Amesley said.

"Something can be done about his scars," Mr. Prior said.

"Garth's going to get plastic surgery as soon as the doctor thinks he's ready. They've already wired his jaw and—But even so, the doctor said there'll always be some scars. Always."

"Well, he's a boy so it won't matter as much," Anna said. She was frowning at Garth, who had stretched out on his stomach on the dirty tile floor and was peeking slyly over his shoulder at his sister.

"Guilt is serving neither you nor your brother well, Lindsay," Mr. Prior said. "You're spoiling him when you let him get away with misbehavior, and for that you *are* responsible."

They didn't understand, Lindsay thought. They simply didn't. She picked Garth up from the floor. "I have to go," she told the others, and without remembering to thank them, she led Garth into their own apartment.

chapter

7

Dad finally had an evening off and it was like the old fun times in Schuylerville. First, he chased Mom from the kitchen. "Go lie down, Faith," he said. "The bags under your eyes are purple."

"Thanks for the compliment," Mom answered him with mild sarcasm. "You making us your famous pasta tonight?"

"Natch," Dad said. "And Lindsay and Garth can help me set the table. Here, Garth, catch." Dad pretended to sail a plate from the dish closet to his son, who crouched in such a good imitation of a catcher that Dad said, "Look at that kid. What'd I tell you? He's a born baseball player."

"That's what you said the day we brought him home from the hospital—which was a little early to tell," Mama said. She was smiling, though; Dad always made her smile.

"Here, Lindsay, you catch," Dad said. This time he did skim the plate through the air.

She caught it, barely, and he grinned and said, "Nothing wrong with your reflexes either, kid. Maybe *you'll* be the pro ball player."

"Oh, Daddy!" she said, but she was pleased.

Humming happily, Dad created his pasta with ingredients from the refrigerator—a little zucchini, an onion, some chunks of jack cheese.

Lindsay glanced at Mama, who was sitting on the living room couch near Garth and the TV. To Lindsay's dismay, Mama looked like a thin-faced old lady, wearing her glasses and bent over the torn underwear she was mending.

"Your mother's working too hard," Dad muttered. His eyes had followed Lindsay's.

"She thinks *you* are," Lindsay said.

"Yeah, but I can go ninety miles an hour without burning out. What do you think all these muscles are for?" He flexed his biceps and grinned at her. "You take after me, honey. We're built for endurance."

"Right," she said, liking to think of herself as strong.

"So how are you taking to city life?" he asked her.

The question shook her. She couldn't think of a positive way to answer it. Carefully, she said, "I miss Schuylerville."

"Have you made any friends?"

"There's no girls my age here, Dad. Besides, I've got to watch Garth."

"Yeah," he said. "I guess it's not like it was in the country. Well, I'll make it up to you once I get a job. Buy you a new bike maybe. How'd you like that?"

"I don't know," she said. A new bike couldn't replace Rona or turn the city streets into pastures. Nor was Mama likely to let her ride a bike in city traffic.

"And when school starts, your brother will go to that day-care place and you'll be free."

Lindsay nodded. Except that she'd have to take care of Garth after school until Mama got home, here in this dingy apartment where the only greenery was the sad ivy in a courtyard they weren't free to play in.

Dad was stirring the pasta vigorously. "So how's Garth behaving himself?" he asked.

Lindsay chewed on her lower lip. Now was her chance to take Mr. Prior's advice and tell on Garth. And she should. What if Garth ran away again, and this time it didn't come out all right? "Well," she began. "Well, sometimes . . ." But she couldn't do it. The words were so sour. "Why don't you ask him, Dad?"

"Hey, Garth," Dad yelled. "Get your butt in here."

Instantly Garth appeared in the kitchen doorway even though his favorite cartoon character was

74

chortling away on the TV screen. He'd never obey Mama or her that fast, Lindsay thought.

"Garth," she said, "tell Daddy what you did."

"What'd I did?"

"When I was sleeping this morning," she reminded him.

"I climb out the window," Garth said as if he expected to be praised.

"You what?" Dad asked. "Out the living room window? Did you fall?"

"There's bags below our window full of leaves and stuff," Lindsay said.

"And we're on the first floor, Bud," Mama, who must have been listening from the couch, put in. "Did he run out into the street?" she asked Lindsay.

"Not this time," Lindsay said. "This time he went into the lobby and a man let him into his apartment."

Dad grunted and Mom gasped.

"No, it was okay," Lindsay assured them. "Hogan talks to himself, but he's not bad—I don't think. I wish Garth wouldn't run away, though."

"Listen, Garth," Daddy said. "You have to stay with your sister. It's not like in the country. You could get hurt. You stay with your sister, or you'll get a whipping from me, hear?" He raised his hand threateningly.

"I a good boy," Garth protested. He rolled his

lips out and his eyes filled with tears. "I a *good* boy," he insisted.

"Sure," Daddy said, "but you got to prove it."

Garth went over and grabbed his father's leg. Dad reached down and hauled him up with one arm. "Want to help me cook?" he asked.

"We better keep the living room window closed and locked when you're sleeping, Lindsay," Mama said.

Lindsay nodded. Somehow she didn't think it could be that simple, but she didn't want to ruin their evening with any more complaining.

As if he were reading her mind for once, Dad said, "It's a tough time for all of us, Lindsay. But we're in it together, right?"

"Right, Dad."

"You're a great kid," he said, and he gave her one of his bone-crushing, one-armed hugs that meant he loved her dearly. The love was her reward, she felt, for not inflicting her personal miseries on him.

Her room was so dark when Lindsay woke up she couldn't tell if it was morning or the middle of the night. Garth was whacking her arm rhythmically. "Kitty," he said. "I want to play with Kitty."

"Where is she?"

"Outside."

"Okay, Garth. Let me get up."

Garth was already dressed in yesterday's dirty T-shirt and shorts. Lindsay gave him clean clothes and said she wouldn't take him out until he changed. Had Dad's threat last night kept Garth in this morning? More likely the locked window had done it. Garth was too much of an optimist to take threats seriously.

Mama had left Lindsay a bowl of cereal and a note. "I reminded Garth he's got to listen to you, Lindsay. Tell me if he doesn't. Peanut butter sandwiches for lunch until I go shopping. Love, Mama."

Garth's nose was squashed against the window. He was watching Sapphire chase a small white butterfly through the ivy. Sapphire trapped the butterfly under her paw, then lifted the paw and looked as if to see why the butterfly wasn't moving. To Lindsay's surprise, it fluttered off. Sapphire balanced on her hind legs and reached out with her front paws to recapture her prey, but she missed. Suddenly she leaped and twirled like an acrobat. Then, as if her exuberance embarrassed her, she stopped to do a serious wash of her creamy chest with her long, pink tongue.

It tickled Lindsay to watch the cat playing by herself. "Isn't she beautiful, Garth?"

"Funny cat," Garth said.

He ran at Sapphire when they reached the

courtyard, but instead of leaping away from him, Sapphire arched her back and stood her ground. Garth stroked her gently in the thin rays of morning sunshine. Lindsay sat on the bench and the cat crept onto her lap and stretched out the way she'd done on Mr. Prior's knees.

"She likes me, Garth," Lindsay said with delight. It seemed Sapphire felt Lindsay belonged in this apartment house, even if Lindsay didn't.

Hogan strode out of the building muttering to himself as usual. ". . . Could've pulled his ear off," he said. "Banged his stupid head against the bricks. Never call me names. No muscle head's gonna—"

"Hi, Mr. Hogan," Lindsay said. She wanted to be neighborly to show her appreciation for his kindness to Garth yesterday.

Hogan stopped and stared at her without recognition.

"It's a nice day today, isn't it?" she said, giving him time to remember who she was.

He frowned at her as if she were speaking a foreign language. "You live here?" he asked.

"Yes," she said. "I'm Garth's sister. Remember? He was wet and you took him in and taught him how to play pool?"

Hogan's eyes went to Garth, then to the cat. "Here, Raki, here, puss," he said. The cat slipped off Lindsay's lap and scooted to Hogan. He stroked her from head to tail while she thrust her head into his hand and rocked in his caress. Unquestionably, Hogan was her favorite person.

"Why do you call her Raki?" Lindsay asked.

"She's got a mask like a raccoon," Hogan said.

"But her real name's Sapphire," Lindsay said.

"She don't care what she's called," he said. The cat was purring now.

Garth leaned against Hogan's side. Unmindful, Hogan kept caressing the cat. The sun massaged Lindsay's shoulders and she rocked contentedly on the edge of the moment.

Mr. Prior eased his way out of the house wearing his usual sport jacket over an open-necked shirt even though it was already warm out. He leaned on his cane, his lipless mouth drawn up in a smile line. "Good morning," he said. "Looks like another lovely summer day."

Lindsay was smiling back at him when the outside gate squeaked and there was Betty. "I knew that cat would be here this morning," she cackled triumphantly. "Hold it for me now. I brought a sack to take it home in." She advanced on Hogan, who was staring at her in alarm.

"My kitty!" Garth said. He picked up the cat and clutched it to his chest.

"Don't, Garth, you'll get clawed again," Lindsay said. She tried to pry his fingers loose as Sapphire yowled, struggling to get free.

Betty came on with the open canvas sack in her hands.

"You can't do this, Betty," Mr. Prior said. "That's no way to treat a cat."

Just then Sapphire sprang away from Garth, scratching Lindsay in her haste, and somehow, in her attempt to capture the cat, Betty fell on top of Sapphire. "Somebody help me," Betty cried. The cat scrambled out from under her, ran up and over the hedge, and leaped into the street.

"Look what you done, you old witch. Look what you done," Hogan said.

"Why didn't you help me catch it?" she asked him.

"Help you? I'd see you in hell first," Hogan said.

Mr. Prior had reached Betty. Leaning heavily on his cane, he hauled her to her feet with his other hand. "Are you all right?" he asked.

She showed him a finger with a tiny thread of blood on it. "I'm bleeding. The nasty beast scratched me deliberately."

"No, I think you hurt yourself falling."

"And it scratched the girl," Betty pointed. Lindsay's arm was oozing blood down a six-inch line. "That's enough! I'm having that cat put to sleep. Even my sister couldn't object. The animal has turned vicious since it's been running wild."

"You better not kill that cat," Hogan said in a threatening manner.

"And you, Mr. Hogan," Betty squawked. "You get out of my house. Out! Your lease is up at the end of the month and I'm *not* renewing it. I'll return your deposit *after* I check the apartment to see what condition it's in. I suppose you haven't learned to lock it yet."

Hogan called her a name and spat on the ground.

"Immediately!" she screamed. "You leave these premises by tomorrow or I'll press assault charges against you."

"He didn't do anything," Lindsay said.

"Calm down, everybody," Mr. Prior said. "Now, Betty, you don't mean what you're saying. Come inside and let me make you a cup of tea. You can deal with this better after you've relaxed and considered—"

"Shut up, Stuart. Don't you tell me how to behave. You wouldn't still be in this building if you had any gumption. Why do you think I married Martin instead of you? At least *he* had guts."

Mr. Prior subsided. His hands fell together on his cane, and for a moment he stood there quietly before he began nodding to himself as if agreeing with what she'd said.

Hogan had stalked out the front gate. Lindsay suddenly realized Garth was gone. "Not again," she wailed and ran into the street after him.

Had he followed Hogan or the cat? She saw Hogan striding down the avenue toward the car wash. He was probably late for work. She hoped he didn't get in trouble for that, too. Garth wasn't chasing after Hogan. He must have followed the cat, then. But where had Sapphire gone?

Traffic was heavy this early in the morning, and for once there were people dressed for work and carrying purses and lunch boxes at the bus stop. But neither Garth nor Sapphire was among them.

Mr. Prior appeared with Betty beside him. "Did you check the alley to see if the little boy ran in there?" Betty asked.

Desperately Lindsay explored the narrow dirt alleyway between the two apartment buildings. It was littered with newspapers, broken bottles, and discarded fast-food containers. Then she saw Garth standing in front of the high fence that blocked the end of the alley. "Garth!" she called.

"Kitty." He pointed up.

"Garth, you ran away again," she said sadly.

"Kitty ran away."

"You didn't listen to me," Lindsay said. "Now I've *got* to punish you."

He frowned at her in warning.

But she was determined. "Come on," she said and took his hand. She walked him past the old people, back into the courtyard, and through the lobby to their apartment. On the way she was thinking hard. Dad would spank Garth, but she couldn't do that. Mama would deprive him of some treat like the Tootsie Pops he loved, or dessert, or his morning television shows. What could she do?

Keep him inside all day. That was the only punishment she could manage. She washed her scratch with soap and water. Then she told Garth to play by himself. To prove she meant to ignore him, she took out her bear collection and laid out her costume materials on the table where the family ate their meals—cloth, buttons and braid, bits of colored foil and lace. She wanted to make another costume as special as the mailman's that Mama so loved, but her mind kept straying. Had Betty meant what she said? Could Mr. Prior talk her out of it? To destroy Sapphire just because of a little scratch—surely nobody could be that cruel.

As if he'd already forgotten he was being punished, Garth lugged his box of toys to Lindsay. "Play with me," he said sweetly.

"No, Garth. You ran away again, so you have to play by yourself."

"You're mean." When his glare didn't move her, he began throwing his toys all over the room.

"Stop that," she told him. "You're being bad, Garth."

"No, you bad. I go outside. Look for Kitty."

"Garth, you ran away, so now you can't go outside."

"No. I look for Kitty before." He stamped his foot.

Actually, she thought, he was right. He had been looking for the cat rather than running away. "But you should have asked me first," she said.

"Play," he demanded and tugged at her shorts.

Furiously he tried to yank the bear out of her hand. "You bad." His angry eyes accused her.

"I'm not the bad one," she said. "You are."

"I hate you," he said.

That scored a direct hit and she lost control. "So what! I hate you, too!" she yelled. And it was true for that instant, but guilt flooded her immediately. Did she hate him? Had she always hated him? Had she secretly wanted him to get hurt? The sly questions dug into her.

He had frozen in shock at her attack. Now he dissolved into wails so loud she was sure the whole apartment house, possibly the whole neighborhood, could hear him. He went on howling until she couldn't stand any more and raised her hand to strike him. But there was the deformed mouth, the monster mask that was her fault.

"All right, all right, Garth. Stop crying, I'll take you outside," she said. "But for just a little while, and you have to stay in the courtyard."

Late that afternoon when Lindsay gave him his bath, she said, "Garth, I love you."

He patted her cheek, leaving a pompom of soap bubbles on it. After he had gotten dressed, they went to the courtyard to sit on the bench and wait for Mama. Lindsay sang all the verses of "Old Mac-Donald." Garth chimed in with the animal sounds and giggled because he thought they were so funny.

The first people through the gate were Amesley and Anna with their jeans-clad mother. "Hear you had a big fight with Mr. Prior's old girlfriend this morning," Amesley said to Lindsay. He was carrying two loaded shopping bags for his mother, whose arm was around Anna.

"Who told you?" Lindsay asked.

"Mr. Prior."

"Kitty ran 'way," Garth said.

"Don't worry, she'll come back. Cats do like that," Amesley said.

"But Betty said she'd have her put down," Lindsay said.

"Her sister's cat? Nah, she wouldn't," Amesley said.

"She might," Anna said. She and her mother had stopped to listen. "So did your sister punish you, Garth?" Anna asked.

"No," Garth said.

"She should have. You're bad to run away all the time," Anna said.

Garth rolled his lips out at her.

"I did punish him. I kept him in the house . . . some," Lindsay said.

"It mustn't have been long enough if he doesn't remember," Anna said.

"This one knows," her mother said, hugging Anna. "She'd make a better teacher than me."

"Too bossy," Amesley said.

"I am not bossy," Anna protested.

"Come on, you two. Do your fighting behind your own walls." Mrs. Blake shoved them both toward the lobby.

Sapphire hadn't reappeared by the time Mama came home, and Hogan hadn't returned either. Lindsay wondered if the landlady had really meant to kick him out and if he had already gone forever. It might be better for Sapphire if she were gone permanently, too—better than landing in Betty's clutches anyway.

When Mama asked how Garth had been, Lindsay said, "Fine." She just couldn't bring herself to tell on him two days in a row. But she wasn't looking forward to tomorrow.

chapter

$$\boxed{8}$$

Saturday morning Mama was very apologetic about breaking her promise to take Lindsay and Garth to the playground. She had to fill in at the post office for someone who was sick and Dad had a special workshop to attend. Lindsay had so looked forward all week to getting Garth to the playground that she said, "Mama, you could let us go alone. Anna and Amesley walk there alone every day."

Mama's eyes grew thoughtful. "You're having a hard time keeping Garth busy in the courtyard, aren't you?"

"Well, he can't do much out there."

With a sigh, Mama said, "Tell you what. See if you can go with the twins and come home with them. That should be safe enough."

"I'll ask them," Lindsay said happily. And, happily, they agreed.

The sky was as gray as the concrete sidewalk, but Lindsay didn't care if it rained. She was glad to be going somewhere, and Garth was thrilled to be going anywhere with Amesley. He skipped beside the older boy, swinging hands with him and ignoring Anna and Lindsay. It was like an adventure, Lindsay thought. Her only exploration of the city streets had been when Garth had run away, and then she'd concentrated too hard on finding him to notice much.

They passed a car that had been stripped of its wheels and abandoned at the curb, an old man lying curled up around a bottle in a paper bag at the entrance to an empty store, an abandoned doll carriage, and two queen-sized ladies in plaid shorts wheeling shopping carts out of the mini-market. Lindsay kept her eyes open for Sapphire. The cat hadn't returned to the house yet. Neither had Hogan as far as she knew.

The playground had been newly built, according to the sign on the cyclone fence around it. Toddlers scurried over the swings and slides and the manual merry-go-round while a few stray adults watched them. Garth crowed in delight at the giant sandbox. He leaped in, scattering little kids to the left and right, and settled down to some serious digging.

Lindsay looked longingly at the parallel bars. Did she dare to take her eyes off Garth and go practice a few gymnastics moves? Amesley was talking to some teenage boys outside the playground, and Anna had plunked herself onto a bench in the shade of the building next to the playground and was already absorbed in a mystery story. Glancing back at Garth, Lindsay saw him reaching out to pet the dandelion-fluff hair of a toddler as if she were the cat. Instantly the child screeched and scrambled away from him to hide her face against the blue-jeaned legs of a boy near Lindsay's age.

"Leave my sister alone, you," the boy said to Garth. "And get your ugly mug out of this sandbox."

Garth didn't budge.

Lindsay rushed to his aid. "He wasn't going to hurt her," she told the boy.

"He's scaring her with his face," the kid said.

"It's better looking than yours," Amesley said. He had come up behind Lindsay.

The boy tightened his fists. His eyes went from Amesley to Lindsay, calculating their strength. Finally he said, "Come on, Sarah. I'll push you on the swing," and he carried the little girl off.

"Garth?" Lindsay questioned. She got down on her knees and looked into his eyes. "You okay?"

Tentatively he put his fingers over his mouth as if to feel the scars. Lindsay choked up. She hugged Garth to her and whispered, "That boy was stupid, Garth. He was so stupid he made me sick."

89

For a minute Garth leaned into her. Then he pushed her away. "I dig," he said and returned to business.

"Your brother's never gonna be the one kids pick on, that's for sure," Anna observed from her bench.

"What do you mean?"

"He's tough," Anna said. "A lot tougher than you, Lindsay."

Later, when the boy and his baby sister had left the park, Amesley took Garth to the swings, and with Garth between his legs squealing joyfully, he pumped the swing until they were both wheeling through the high blue sky.

"Amesley's so good with my brother," Lindsay said to Anna.

"You'd be good with him, too, if you learned to say no to him like you meant it," Anna lectured her. "You're such a sofa pillow, Lindsay. It's no wonder he thinks he can do what he wants."

"He used to listen to me," Lindsay said.

"When? You mean before the horseshoe hit him? That should tell you to stop being sorry for him and get tough again."

"I can't." Lindsay's stomach churned as she remembered Garth's sudden awareness of his face after that boy insulted him. And if the scars weren't fixed enough when he went to school? Someday Garth can wear a beard, the doctor had said, but a beard wouldn't hide his face in elementary school.

What if kids didn't want to be his friends? What if he started feeling bad about himself? Lindsay twisted her shoulders and bit her lip, suffering for him in advance.

"I wish it had been me," she burst out. Then she flushed, embarrassed at saying what she wasn't sure she really meant.

"I know what!" Anna snapped her fingers as if she'd just made a discovery.

"What?"

"I just remembered something the preacher said in church last Sunday. It's like he was talking about you, and it gives me an idea."

"Tell me."

"No. First, I've got to talk to Amesley and see what Mr. Prior says." Anna set her book down and stared straight ahead of her. "You go ahead and play. I'll watch Garth for a while."

Lindsay wanted to protest Anna's treating her like a child again, but instead she swallowed her anger and walked over to the parallel bars. There she began practicing her pullovers. It was a pleasure to swing her body through gymnastics exercises and find she still had her elastic strength even though she hadn't practiced since school ended. She did some forward rolls, vaguely aware that she had an admiring audience of two kindergarten-age girls. Suddenly she noticed Anna and Amesley watching her. She didn't want them to think she was showing off, so she completed a couple of head-stands and a handstand and stopped.

"Hey, Lindsay, you're good!" Amesley said. "Can you do a back flip?"

"I guess," she said and showed him.

The little girls clapped. Lindsay said, "It's not hard."

Garth charged into Amesley, nearly knocking him down. "Play with me, guy," Garth yelled.

Amesley pretended to wrestle with him. Then he said, "Oh, no, short stuff, you're too much for me. I give up. I surrender. You win."

"No." Garth stopped struggling and put his arms around Amesley. "You win. You the best."

Amesley laughed, hugged Garth, and swung him around in a circle.

The instant he was set down, Garth took Amesley's hand and dragged him off to the manual merry-go-round. A bunch of scruffy little kids were making it spin. Several of them greeted Amesley by name.

Lindsay drifted back to the bench where Anna had returned to her reading. She looked up from her book inquiringly.

"Amesley knows a lot of people," Lindsay said.

"Amesley's friends with the whole world," Anna said scornfully. "That's why Ma doesn't trust him and makes us buddy up all the time. He'd get in with a bad crowd for sure without me around."

"These kids don't look bad."

"These are the babies. You go out in the street sometime when the gangs are out. Our neighborhood gang's the Rap Tops. They're not as bad as some, but you can't join them unless you get cut in a fight. They asked Amesley to join, but Ma said if he got himself cut, she'd chop off her own finger. She would, too. Ma's fierce."

"Do you have friends here in the park, Anna?" Lindsay asked.

"I say hi to a couple of kids, but they're not my friends. Mostly I come here for the crafts stuff or I read."

"What about in school?" Lindsay asked.

Anna wrinkled her nose. "Nobody in *my* class I'd pick for a friend. Seems like they're trashy or brainless or both."

"But Anna—" Don't you get lonely, was what Lindsay wanted to ask, but she held her tongue in case the question might hurt Anna's feelings.

"What?" Anna demanded. Her hair was done in tight braids today and her plain face looked polished.

"Do you just have Amesley and your mother? I mean, don't you have a father or anybody?" Lindsay heard herself ask.

"No father. Ma says we don't need one. She says she hasn't met the man yet good enough to bring up her children." Anna said it proudly.

"Really?" It surprised Lindsay that a woman might choose a man for his potential as a parent. Mama hadn't picked Dad that way. She'd fallen in love with him riding on the back of his motorcycle with her arms wrapped around his chest and her cheek against his leather jacket. At least, that was what Dad claimed.

"Ma says raising children is more important than any other job, and she aims to do it right," Anna was saying. "My mother is the best."

"She looks nice," Lindsay said, thinking of the smile that Ms. Blake wore as an everyday garment.

For a minute they watched Amesley and Garth on the merry-go-round. Then Lindsay said, "I guess Mr. Prior couldn't talk the landlady into letting Hogan stay."

"Hogan didn't give him a chance," Anna said. "He's gone. He left his plant in front of our door with a note stuck in it asking us to feed the cat."

"No kidding? But the cat's gone, too."

"Maybe. Amesley thinks somebody in the neighborhood could have adopted Toasty because she's so pretty," Anna said.

Lindsay felt bad about the cat being lost, just when she was becoming a friend. Hogan, too. Lindsay wished they'd both come back.

A soccer ball some kids had been playing with rolled against Anna's leg. She sent it flying back to them with an impatient kick.

Hopefully Lindsay offered, "Well, Mr. Prior says she's been gone for days before and come back."

"Mr. Prior always thinks everything's going to come out right." Anna was sounding scornful again. "Just like in those little kids' stories he made about animals finding a home and friends? The library has a shelf full of them, but nobody reads them anymore."

"Well, things do come out right sometimes," Lindsay said stubbornly. "I like Mr. Prior. As soon as I get to the library, I'm going to get some of his books to read to Garth."

"I bet you Garth won't listen. Mr. Prior's books are too old-fashioned. Tell you what, I'll get some for you when Ma takes us to the library this after-noon."

"Would you? That would be really nice, Anna." Lindsay didn't expect her parents would have time to take her. And when Anna came with the books, Lindsay could show her her bear collection. Anna liked doing crafts, so she might be interested.

Idly Lindsay wondered if Anna had forgotten whatever idea she had had earlier about Lindsay, or if she still intended to consult Amesley and Mr. Prior about it.

On the way home from the playground, Lindsay again kept an eye out for Sapphire, but the only animal she saw was an old dog walking himself from telephone pole to hydrant and back.

❦

Rona called while Lindsay was making lunch for Garth.

"Lindsay, Jill got you a poster you're just going to love for your birthday, but she won't be around to give it to you because guess what?"

"What?"

"Her dad bought a camper and they've taken off to visit relatives for a whole month. She'll miss your party, but she left the poster with me to give you."

"What'll you do without her around, Rona?"

"Oh, you know, help out at my folks' vegetable stand and stuff . . . I'm really looking forward to your party, Lindsay."

"Me, too." Rona would never guess how much.

"So did you make any friends yet?"

"Not yet," Lindsay said. "The people here are nice, but there's no girls my age."

"There's a kid that moved into your house," Rona told her. "She's kind of quiet, like you, but she's not good at athletic stuff." Rona sighed. "I wish you could go bike riding with me this afternoon."

"Well, next week when I come to Schuylerville for my birthday, maybe we can go bike riding *and* play miniature golf," Lindsay said. She was thinking that if Rona got lonely enough, she'd make friends with the new girl.

The thought left her feeling jealous instead of comforted when the phone call was over.

Then Anna came by with the books, and Lindsay invited her to come in.

"I can't right now. Sorry," Anna said.

Lindsay thanked her for the books and collected Garth from the TV. "I'm going to read to you now," she said with determination. She wanted to read to him so she wouldn't have to sit and think about how lonely she was.

The first book was about a mouse who was furnishing his bachelor quarters with things that were important to him, like a handknitted blanket and a pillow stuffed with juniper berries and a china thimble just the right size to use as a teacup. Garth listened quietly through about half the book before he got restless and wandered off to find his dump truck. Lindsay paged slowly through the rest of the pictures, admiring the loving detail that Mr. Prior had put into every illustration. Why didn't kids like his books anymore? They should, she thought, and when she saw him, she'd tell him so.

A few minutes later, Dad burst into the apartment demanding to know what they had to eat. Lindsay fixed him a leftover chicken sandwich with a slathering of mayonnaise, the way he liked it.

"You're a great cook, honey girl," he said.

"Mama cooked the chicken," she informed him.

"But you made the sandwich. What say we clean the house to surprise our working woman?"

"Yeah!" Garth said, and Lindsay nodded with equal enthusiasm. Cleaning house with Dad could be exciting. One time they had slid around the bare parts of floors with dust rags tied to their feet. Usually they sang as they cleaned.

It was a treat to see Mama's pleasure when she got home and found the kitchen floor still wet from washing. Later, when Mama asked how it had gone at the playground, Lindsay didn't mention the boy who'd made Garth feel bad. After she'd told Mama all the good things that had happened, Mama said, "I guess it would be all right for you to take Garth to the playground by yourself sometimes."

While things were going her way, Lindsay asked, "Mama, if the landlady's cat comes back, can we take her in?"

"No, Lindsay, not without her permission. After all, it's her cat."

"It was her *sister's* cat."

"Well, now it's hers. You can't just take somebody's pet from them. That's stealing."

"We'll get you your own cat one of these days," Dad said from the couch where he was trying to study.

"Maybe we could buy Sapphire," Lindsay persisted.

"Not likely. Siamese cats are expensive," Mama

said. "Besides, that one's too independent to make a good pet."

Lindsay didn't argue, but she was sure Mama was wrong. Sapphire liked people, and she'd be a wonderful pet. But first, she had to be found.

chapter

9

Sunday was a pearly, perfect summer day. Lindsay sat dreamily on Mr. Prior's bench in the courtyard wondering where Sapphire could be and wishing she'd return. Amesley and Anna came out of the house with their mother, all of them dressed up for church. It was the first time Lindsay had seen their mother in anything but jeans.

"You look pretty, Ms. Blake," she said.

"Thank you, Lindsay. I feel pretty this morning. Smell that sweet summer air!" Ms. Blake took a deep breath. "You'd think we were in the country." Her dress was printed with daisies and her high-heeled sandals were green. Anna wore a baggy white cotton dress as plain as her face.

"Don't I look good, too?" Amesley asked. He had on multicolor pants and a sparkling white shirt that contrasted well with his mocha-colored skin.

Lindsay nodded, too shy to say what she thought,

which was that Amesley always looked good because his smile dressed up his face so well.

"So where's short stuff this morning?" Amesley asked.

"Mama's cutting his hair." Just as Lindsay said it, a howl issued from the apartment.

Amesley laughed. "Sounds like she's cutting his throat."

"Mama can handle him," Lindsay said.

"Probably because she doesn't give in to him all the time," Anna said.

"Children take advantage if you let them," Ms. Blake said in agreement with her daughter.

"I guess." Lindsay folded in her lips, trying to hide that their comments had pushed her close to tears. Lately it seemed she came close to tears often. It disgusted her to have gotten so weak.

"We're going to toughen Lindsay up," Anna said as if she were reading Lindsay's mind.

"How are you going to do that, Anna baby?" her mother asked.

"Don't worry, Ma," Anna said. "We're not going to do anything bad." She smiled at Lindsay so that Lindsay knew Anna must be referring to the idea she'd had at the playground. What could Anna possibly have in mind? Something magical? Something that would transform Lindsay and make her strong again? But Anna was only a couple of years older. How could she be that wise?

"This afternoon Mama's watching Garth,"

Lindsay said to change the subject, "and I thought I'd go looking for Sapphire."

"Wait till I'm back from church and I'll go with you," Amesley offered.

"Would you? That would be great," Lindsay said.

Soon after they left, Mr. Prior came out. "Ah, the good sun," he said as he eased himself onto the bench beside Lindsay. He looked fragile as an empty eggshell to her this morning.

"What's the longest time Sapphire's been gone?" Lindsay asked him.

"I can't say I've ever kept count. A week maybe."

"Do you think she'll come back, Mr. Prior?"

"I hope she will. This courtyard's not the same without her, is it?"

"No," Lindsay said. In fact, the courtyard seemed strangely lifeless without the cat, as if Sapphire were its resident spirit.

"When Amesley gets back from church, he's going with me to look for Sapphire," she said. "Want to come, too, Mr. Prior?"

"Why, I'd be happy to accompany you." Mr. Prior sounded pleased to be asked. "Maybe we'll come across poor Hogan while we're at it."

"I can't believe Betty kicked him out."

"It would be more accurate to say that Hogan kicked himself out. He's a sensitive man and Betty offended his dignity."

"Is it true that you wanted to marry her, Mr. Prior?" Lindsay asked.

He nodded. "Betty was the most enchanting young woman. It broke my heart when she refused me." He laughed. "Strange how often one doesn't recognize one's good fortune."

"You mean you're glad she said no?"

"Well, some people are best loved at a distance. Betty would have been difficult for a man like me to live with."

"But you stayed here anyway, even though she married someone else."

"Yes," he said. "Yes, I did. I guess I have the story-teller's habit of wanting to see how things turn out." He nodded. "They were a pair of scrappers, she and Martin. It's a wonder they didn't kill each other." He chuckled and nodded his head.

"Was he your friend, too?"

"Oh, yes. We all went to school together sixty-odd years ago." He shook his head in wonder. "Isn't it amazing that life should remain so interesting whether it comes out badly or well? I suspect it's the element of surprise that does it."

A breeze flipped up the leaves above her head. Lindsay said, "I read one of your books to Garth, Mr. Prior."

"Did you?" He gave her a wary glance. "I don't suppose it was his kind of reading material."

"Oh, yes. He loved it," Lindsay said quickly. "And so did I."

"Is that so?" Mr. Prior sat up straighter and a bit of color came into his cheeks. "Well, that's good to hear. That's really good to hear. Perhaps it's too soon for me to be thinking of giving up after all."

"Do you make up new books all the time? I mean, do you work on them every day?" Lindsay asked.

"Every day," he said. "That's mainly what my life is about, Lindsay."

"Well, then you can't give up, can you?"

He laughed. "I suppose not. I suppose I really can't." The discovery seemed to delight him.

An hour later, while Anna was helping her mother cook Sunday dinner and Mama was watching Garth, Lindsay and Amesley and Mr. Prior made a circuit of the neighborhood as they searched for Sapphire.

Lindsay noticed a small boy about Garth's age in the chain of small, identical private houses in the street behind theirs. The child's slim father had his head bound in a funny turban with a topknot. Lindsay tried not to stare at it while the man told Mr. Prior in musically accented English that he hadn't seen the cat they described, but he would keep an eye out for it.

"Pleasant fellow. I'd guess from his headgear that he's a Sikh. From India, you know," Mr. Prior said when they were on their way again.

Lindsay wondered if Mama would let her walk

around the block with Garth to make friends with the Sikh-from-India's son. It would be good for Garth to play with someone his own age.

A plump young woman in a shiny, skintight aerobics workout outfit was exercising to music from a tape deck on an apron of concrete in front of her house. "Your turn to inquire about the cat, Amesley," Mr. Prior said.

"Not me," Amesley said. "That's Alfrieda. She's got it in for men, and she don't trust boys much either."

"I'll ask her," Lindsay offered.

The woman, Alfrieda, didn't miss a beat of her exercising as she answered Lindsay. "There's a zillion cats around here." One knee and then the other met alternate elbows as she spoke. "Just leave off a garbage can lid and you'll get your pick."

"But Sapphire's a Siamese," Lindsay said.

"So? I saw an Angora the other day. Cats won't be loyal. Get yourself a dog." When she began counting loudly, Lindsay backed off.

Three-quarters of the way around the block, Amesley hailed some boys on skateboards. "Hey, Louie, lemme have a turn?" he begged.

Mr. Prior, who was looking very weary, said, "I think I'd best head for home now."

Lindsay walked back with him, leaving Amesley with his friends. "It's not such a bad neighborhood," she said, despite what Anna had told her.

"Oh, the people here are mostly good, like people everywhere," Mr. Prior said. "But there are characters who traffic in drugs and steal things as well as some troublesome youths who—You need to be careful."

"But you keep on living here," Lindsay said.

Mr. Prior nodded. "It's my home and it would be hard for me to leave," he said. "Did you feel that way about the place you moved from?"

"Yes." His understanding touched Lindsay. "Mr. Prior," she said, "Anna has some kind of idea about me, about Garth and me. She said she was going to talk to you about it. Did she?"

"She proposed something to me that was imaginative, but fairly radical. I said I'd think about it." He studied Lindsay carefully. "How about it? Do you want your friends interfering in your life?"

"Oh, yes," Lindsay said immediately.

It was only much later that she realized the friends Mr. Prior was referring to couldn't be Rona and Jill because he didn't know them. Were Anna and Amesley her friends, then? Was Mr. Prior? He was certainly a dear old man, the oldest person she had ever met, older than her grandparents had been when they died. She guessed he was near eighty. She would have been happy to have him as a grandfather, or a great-grandfather. But as a friend?

She had always thought friends had to be her own age, or close to it. Friends were the people she most wanted to be with when she wasn't with her family. Friends liked to do the same things she did, and they cared about her and she about them. Did all that apply to the people in the apartment house?

Lindsay didn't think so. Anna and Amesley were older and their interests were different from hers. Besides, Amesley, whom she liked best, was a boy, which meant she could never be that close to him— not secrets-telling, silly-acting close. But it was something to think about—what made someone a friend.

chapter

10

The next morning Lindsay was just washing up the breakfast dishes before taking Garth outside when someone rapped loudly on the door. Nobody ever pounded on their door like that. "Who is it?" she asked fearfully.

"It's me. Amesley."

Relieved, she unlocked the door and greeted him with a smile. He was wearing his colorful pants, a white shirt, and a tie.

"What are you all dressed up for?" she asked.

"You!" he said, pointing a finger at her. "We got serious business this morning, Lindsay Carson. I gotta take you to court."

"What?"

"Yeah, you been summoned." He threw his head back and pointed a thumb at himself cockily. "And guess who's your defense attorney."

She shook her head as if to wake herself up.

"I know," he said. "It sounds crazy. But this is Anna's idea, and Mr. Prior agreed to be the judge, so he thinks it's okay. I mean—" Amesley shrugged. "I'm just going along with it because they let me be the good guy."

"But why do I have to go to court?"

"You'll find out. Come on, Garth. We gotta go someplace."

Garth had been watching TV. Now he noticed Amesley, and with a yelp of joy he jumped onto the bigger boy, wrapping his legs around Amesley's waist. Amesley toted him out to the courtyard that way while Lindsay switched off the TV and followed in confusion.

Mr. Prior was seated on the bench in his usual jacket and open-necked shirt. In front of him was a table draped with a black shawl. On it was a pitcher of water, a glass, and something that looked like a gavel, which on closer inspection turned out to be a wooden nutcracker.

"I don't understand what's going on," Lindsay whispered.

"Silence," Anna said sternly. "You're the accused and you can't talk till you're spoken to. I'm the prosecutor." She shone with pride in her role.

"But I don't understand—" Lindsay said again.

"Don't worry; it'll be okay." Amesley patted her back. Comforting as his presence was, Lindsay still felt anxious. Garth was now hanging from Amesley's arm like a shoulder bag.

"Harrumph," Mr. Prior said. "This court is open for business. Will the honorable prosecutor be so kind as to present her case first."

"My case, Your Honor," Anna said smoothly, "is the people versus Lindsay. She's accused of causing her little brother great harm and damage."

"How specifically is she alleged to have damaged her little brother?" Mr. Prior asked. His smooth, nearly chinless face was a solemn mask. Fearfully Lindsay stared at Anna. Even though Lindsay understood that this was a mock trial, probably the acting-out of Anna's "radical" idea, her heart had begun gyrating wildly and she couldn't slow it. She bit her lip and tried to hide her agitation.

Anna said, "The prosecution will prove that Lindsay did willfully and deliberately allow her little brother to run in the path of a horseshoe that hit him in the mouth and messed him up bad."

"The prosecutor has spoken," Mr. Prior said. "Now, defense, will you please state your case." He turned toward Amesley.

"Oh, she didn't do it. She's a good kid. It was just an accident." Amesley spoke so casually that Mr. Prior pursed his lips and frowned at him in warning. Amesley raised his eyebrows in response.

Mr. Prior coughed. "Very well," he said. "Let us

begin. I shall allow the accused to make a statement on her own behalf if that is agreeable with all
parties?"

"It is agreeable, Your Honor," Anna said.

Lindsay's voice quavered as she said, "I don't
have anything to say."

"Do you want to plead guilty?" Mr. Prior asked.

"Well, I don't know," Lindsay said.

"Nah, why should she plead guilty?" Amesley
said. "She didn't do it. She's innocent."

"Are you innocent?" Mr. Prior asked Lindsay
with a peculiar intensity.

She shook her head, strangling on her dismay.

Everyone stared at her in a silence that lasted
too long.

Finally, Mr. Prior said, "Why don't you present
your case against her now, prosecutor?"

"All right, Your Honor," Anna said. "First off,
she's big and the kid, as you can see, is little. He
was even littler when his mouth got bashed in."

Lindsay winced. Garth grinned as if he liked
being the center of attention.

"So obviously, she could have held on to him if
she'd really wanted to," Anna continued. "She
must have been mad at him to let go at just the
wrong minute." Anna put her finger to her lips
thoughtfully. "Or . . ." she said, as if what followed
might be a revelation, "maybe she was jealous of
the kid because he was a boy baby and got the

most attention." Her eyes surveyed them triumphantly, but nobody seemed to be reacting. "Anyway," she concluded after giving them another few seconds to absorb her wisdom, "the fact is, Lindsay Carson could have held on to her little brother and she didn't."

Mr. Prior turned toward Garth, then to Amesley. "What do you say to that, Mister Defender?"

"Hey, this little kid's strong," Amesley began. "He'll wiggle off in a second if you give him any slack. Like, say you want to smack a mosquito or look over your shoulder at something? Bam, he's gone like a shot." Amesley slapped one palm off the other. "Right, short stuff?"

"Right, guy," Garth said. As if to illustrate, he broke away from Amesley and dashed toward the gate.

"Hey, Garth, come back here! You can't leave the court without the judge's permission," Amesley yelled. In three long steps, he'd caught up with Garth, and he carried the giggling boy back to face Mr. Prior.

"I would say that the defense has proven its point," Mr. Prior said. "What does the prosecution have to say?"

"Lindsay, did you let go of him because you were hitting a mosquito or looking over your shoulder?" Anna asked.

"No, I don't think so."

"Then why *did* you let go of him?"

"I don't know." She shuddered.

"Sure, you know. Think about it. Were you mad because you had to take care of him?" Anna asked. "Were you jealous of him?" She leaned insistently toward Lindsay.

Lindsay drew back and swallowed. Her mouth was dry and her insides were in such a turmoil that it was hard to think. Besides, she'd avoided remembering that day for so long that now it was hard to recall it. Whenever her mind had dragged it up, she'd closed her eyes and held her hands over her ears to shut out the images. The hurt had been unbearable—her hurt, because it had happened to her, too.

It had been hot for April, hotter than it had gotten yet in the city this summer. She'd been wearing shorts with her bathing suit underneath because the bathing suit was old and too small for her. When the men started pitching horseshoes, she'd seen Garth wander over to them and she'd gone after him. It had been her own idea to follow Garth. Yes, now she remembered.

"He went. I didn't take him. He went," Lindsay said out loud.

. . . And she'd sat down on a mound of hay with Garth in her lap to watch the men. He was plump and his skin smelled sweet even though most everyone was perspiring in the heat, even the churchwomen under the shade of the trees packing away the food on the picnic table.

Lindsay had nuzzled Garth's neck. He'd giggled because it tickled him when she did that. She heard the clang of the iron shoe hitting the iron post and the shout of the deacon who had made a ringer.

Then a woman's high voice had yelled something about ice cream. Yes, the ice cream had come late. They'd finished the picnic lunch without it and then a woman had called, "Ice cream, come and get it before it melts."

"He jerked out of my arms," Lindsay said aloud from the center of her remembering. "He wanted the ice cream. He ran right in the path of the horseshoe some man threw." She put her hand over her mouth and closed her eyes, hearing the scream again.

. . . The scream, like an eerie siren full of dread. Then everyone began screaming. Blood had burst from Garth's mouth and made a red beard down his chin. Bodies had hurtled past Lindsay, blocking her sight, and she couldn't even get to her little brother through all the adults who descended on him.

Dad's friend from the lumberyard had asked angrily, "Who was watching the kid? Wasn't anybody watching him?"

"His sister," someone had said. That was when Lindsay had known with a terrible sense of doom that what had happened to Garth had been her fault.

"But I couldn't help it," Lindsay whispered. "It happened too fast."

"There, there," Mr. Prior was saying. "Maybe this wasn't such a good idea. We weren't trying to upset you, Lindsay. We were trying to prove to you that you were innocent. You *are* innocent. What happened to your little brother was not your fault."

"It was an accident," Anna said. "And like our preacher said Sunday, 'Guilt poisons you until you seek forgiveness.'"

Their concern surprised Lindsay until she realized tears were streaming down her cheeks and dripping off her chin. Besides, she was shivering although it was already a hot morning.

"Gee, now look what we did," Amesley said. "See, I told you guys this was a dumb idea."

Garth put his arms around Lindsay. "Don't cry," he begged. "Don't cry, Lindsay." At that she broke down altogether and sank in a heap on the ivy with Garth in her arms.

All that morning she wept. Amesley said he'd take care of Garth, and Anna offered to stay in the apartment with Lindsay, but she said, "No," without explanation and Anna backed off.

Lindsay didn't care if Anna thought she was angry with her. She felt too awful to care about anything but her own pain. She curled up on her bed and cried and cried, mindless tears that wouldn't stop even when she told herself she must stop, that she really had nothing to cry about.

Most likely Anna and Amesley and Mr. Prior had meant to help, not hurt her. But something had gone very wrong and now the tears kept coming in a never-ending flow. Anna should have minded her own business, Lindsay decided. Anna thought she knew so much. And Mr. Prior—Mr. Prior should have known better.

Around noon she ran dry. Garth didn't want to leave Amesley, who was teaching him to play baseball in the courtyard with a plastic bat and ball, but Lindsay was still responsible for her little brother.

"You have to eat lunch, Garth. Come on," she said. When he pretended not to hear her, she said, "Garth, you come now or I'll have to punish you."

"Ho, ho, ho! Listen to her!" Amesley said. "You're sounding like Anna!"

But she wasn't, Lindsay realized. She was sounding like her old self.

After lunch, Lindsay walked Garth over to the playground, but it was too hot, and there was no shade and no one around for him to play with. Garth didn't want to dig.

"I go swim," he said as if she could produce an instant pool of water for him.

"You can't swim," Lindsay said. "We live in the city now, Garth. There's no place to swim."

"Yes there is." He pointed to something she hadn't noticed, an open water hydrant across the street from which a luxuriant stream of water cascaded.

"But we can't go there," Lindsay said.

"Yes." Garth nodded his head and marched toward the street.

She grabbed him by the shoulder. "Mama wouldn't like it if you played in the gutter. We'll go home and you can cool off in the bathtub." He struggled to get loose from her and she held on stubbornly. For once, the guilt didn't settle over her like a fog and immobilize her. She looked at his face without being reminded of how she had failed him and, doggedly, she held on.

Still, it amazed her that he finally gave in and let her walk him home. She listened to him sniveling and thought, is this all I have to do, just not give in? Somehow it seemed familiar, like behavior she had once mastered in the days when she'd been the confident big sister. The days before April when she'd believed in her own goodness.

At home, Lindsay filled the bathtub as she'd promised, and Garth spent a couple of hours playing in it with his boats.

The courtyard was cooler in late afternoon when it was in deep shade.

117

Lindsay sat under the tree and let Garth dig. She wondered where Sapphire was. She wondered where Mr. Prior and Amesley and Anna had gone. She wondered if she should say anything to them about what they'd done to her.

The normal veil of sadness that evening brought with it lay heavy in the shadows of the courtyard. To cheer herself up, Lindsay thought about Saturday. Then she'd be with Rona in Schuylerville for her birthday, and everything would feel right for a change.

chapter

11

The air was so soggy with heat Tuesday morning that Lindsay woke up feeling as if she were wrapped in a wet towel. Everything looked fuzzy, and even though the windows were open, it was hard to breathe. The TV was already chittering away so she knew Garth was awake. She used the bathroom and went to join Mama in the kitchen, pulling Garth back from the screen as she passed him.

"It's going to be a hot one," Mama said. She poured a glass of juice for Lindsay, then pushed the sticky hair back from her daughter's face with thin, cool fingers. "If it's this muggy tonight, we'll go have supper at a mall to cool off." Mama's eyes were melting as she added, "I'm sorry you're stuck here. I wish I could take you and Garth to the post office with me. There may not be any windows, but the air conditioning works fine."

"It's okay, Mama. Garth doesn't mind the heat. We'll go to the playground," Lindsay said.

"I never wanted to put so much responsibility on you, Lindsay," Mama said. "I meant for you to have a real childhood."

"Mama, it's okay. I don't mind." Today reassuring Mama came easily. It *was* okay. Yesterday's crying jag had somehow leached out Lindsay's fears and left her more confident that she could deal with her obstreperous little brother. Even her anger at Anna and Mr. Prior had cooled overnight.

After Mama went to work, Lindsay studied the courtyard. It was so saturated with sunshine that it looked hot and uninviting. In the country she could fill Garth's plastic pool, or they could spray each other with the hose. Here there was only the bathtub. Then she remembered Dad had brought home a bag of balloons the other night. "Want to throw water balloons, Garth?"

Did he ever! She couldn't fill the balloons fast enough for him. He squealed as he gleefully pitched each one into the empty courtyard. He was tossing out a big red one just as Betty stepped through the gate dressed in white pants and a pink shirt.

Despite her wizened face, Betty looked almost pretty to Lindsay today—until she yelled, "Why are you letting that child mess up my courtyard?"

"But it's only water," Lindsay said. "It won't hurt anything and I'll pick up the balloons." Garth ducked below the window and crawled off to hide behind the couch.

"You better pick them up," Betty said. "Has Mr. Hogan come back?"

"I haven't seen him," Lindsay said.

"Well, I'm going up to check his apartment. But first—I don't suppose you've seen my cat, either, have you?"

Lindsay shook her head.

Betty sniffed. "As if you'd tell me! I know you people think it's a big joke to hide that cat from me, but you'll see. I'll get it back without your help. . . . Here, boy." She beckoned.

A thin Asian boy in his late teens slipped into the courtyard. He was dressed in ill-fitting jeans and a baggy white T-shirt and clutched a folding chair, a long-handled net, and a cat carrying cage.

"This is where you sit to watch for the cat," Betty told him.

He peered at her anxiously from under a ragged fringe of black hair.

"Here." Betty raised her voice and pointed at the ground. "Meow, meow," she said. Impatiently she dug a photo out of her purse and stabbed her finger at it. "Cat," she said.

The boy shrank back as if the picture or Betty or both frightened him.

"Oh, for pity's sake," Betty said. "You'd think they could send me an English-speaking boy." She glared at him. Suddenly she yanked the chair from his hand, set it down, took a bill from her wallet and waved it at him. His eyes brightened at the sight of the money. She showed him the photo again and pointed to the cage. "Catch cat. Understand? Catch *my* cat."

He nodded, and sat down in the chair in a patch of sunlight with the net and the cage beside him. His eyes yearned after the bill as Betty returned it to her wallet.

She glanced at Lindsay in the window. "Has Mr. Prior come out yet?"

"I haven't seen him this morning," Lindsay said.

"Well, it *is* hot. I better go tell him to keep an eye on this boy." As she was about to step into the house, she turned and asked, "How's your scratch?"

"Okay."

"Is it? *I'm* still sore from where that beast dug its claws into me."

"Sapphire's really a sweet cat."

"Sweet? Don't be ridiculous. Cats are sly, selfish creatures with no affection for anyone but themselves. And this one has become a menace." Betty raised her hand as if Lindsay might protest. "Never mind. It's too hot to argue. Just clean up this mess while I go talk to Stuart."

Betty stalked into the house on her high heels and Lindsay climbed out the window over the now well-squashed bags. She picked up the multi-colored balloons, most of which were still intact and could be filled and thrown again as soon as Betty had taken her disagreeable self away.

The Asian boy was watching glumly. Lindsay thought he'd get heat stroke sitting there in the sun instead of in the shade under the tree. She got him a glass of water from the kitchen, but he wouldn't leave the chair to take it when she held the glass out the window to him. Once more, she climbed out so that she could put the glass in his hand. He said something she didn't understand. Then he tasted the water, smiled at her, and drank it all down.

"Who's he?" Garth said. He was standing at Lindsay's heels.

"The landlady's catcatcher," Lindsay said. "Who said you could come out, Garth?"

"You're out."

"But who said you could? You're supposed to ask me. Got that?"

"Got it," he said.

Betty suddenly emerged from the lobby. "You, girl," she called urgently to Lindsay. "Mr. Prior's had a heart attack. I've called for an ambulance. Can you show them the way to his apartment when they get here?"

Lindsay caught her breath in dismay before she said, "Yes, sure. Is Mr. Prior—?"

"He's still alive, thank heavens." Betty's eyes filled with tears and she hurried back inside.

The siren announced the arrival of the ambulance crew a few minutes later. Lindsay led them through the courtyard where Garth was trying unsuccessfully to get the catcatcher to play ball with him. It seemed a long time before she saw Mr. Prior being carried out on a stretcher. The part of his normally pale face that wasn't covered by an oxygen mask was a glassy white. Lindsay's heart lurched. Why hadn't she gotten around to telling him what a dear, dear man she thought he was? "Please get well, Mr. Prior," she called as he disappeared through the gate with Betty bustling along beside him.

The catcatcher sat on in his chair gaping after them in bewilderment.

Later in the afternoon the courtyard was in shade, still hot but less oppressively so. Lindsay brought the boy, who hadn't moved, another drink and a peach. He smiled. Then he said something in his own language that she took to be a thank you.

"You're welcome," she said.

The minute Amesley and Anna stepped through the gate, Lindsay gave them the news about Mr. Prior. "Where were you?" she asked, as if their being present would have made a difference.

"Our church youth group went to that park

across the river to swim," Anna said. "Do you know what hospital they took Mr. Prior to?"

"I can't believe he got a heart attack," Amesley said. "That sucks."

"We could ask Betty where he is and how he's doing," Lindsay said.

"If he's still alive, we can send him a get-well card," Anna said.

"Whaddaya mean if he's still alive?" Amesley said. "What kind of talk is that? Mr. Prior's a neat guy. He'll get well. Sure he will."

Anna raised an eyebrow at her brother. "He's pretty old, Amesley."

"Nah, he's just lived a long time. That doesn't make him old. *You're* old, Anna, not him." Amesley sounded agitated.

Anna sniffed and turned her back on her brother without answering him. Instead she asked Lindsay who the kid in the chair was.

"You mean he hasn't got up to go to the bathroom all day?" Amesley asked after Lindsay had explained.

"I think he's too scared of Betty to move," Lindsay said.

"That figures. But what if Betty's forgotten him?" Amesley went over to the boy and did a pantomime which they couldn't see because his back was toward them. The boy stood up and followed Amesley into the house.

Anna shook her head. "Good thing Toasty is gone. I hope she doesn't come back while that kid is here. I wouldn't put it past Betty to have her put down. . . . About yesterday, Lindsay," Anna said. "The trial? I was just trying to help, you know."

The last remnant of Lindsay's resentment was wiped out by Anna's apology. "I know you were," Lindsay said. Actually, it was beginning to seem that Anna had helped. Radical, Mr. Prior had said—Anna had had a radical idea. That meant far out. And it had been painful. But feeling so bad seemed to have let Lindsay start feeling good again.

Mama kept her promise that evening and took Lindsay and Garth to the food court of an air-conditioned mall for tacos. The catcatcher wasn't in the courtyard when they came home, although his chair and net and cage remained. To please Lindsay, Mama called up the two hospitals in town and located Mr. Prior at the main one.

"They said he's in the cardiac care unit and no one can see him," Mama told Lindsay.

"But did they say how he was?"

"He can't be too good if he's in cardiac care, but at least he's still alive."

✛

Anna knocked at their door the next morning. She also had found out where Mr. Prior was. "Want to come to my apartment and help Amesley and me make get-well cards for Mr. Prior?" Anna asked. "Garth can come, too."

Garth was eager to go anywhere that Amesley was, so Lindsay took him up to the Blakes' apartment and the four of them set to work around a big maple table.

Garth spent all of five seconds scribbling on the outside of a piece of folded colored paper before saying, "All done. I play now."

Amesley gave him a box of his own old toys, mostly plastic figures of spacemen and animals. That kept Garth busy while the rest of them worked on their cards.

A few minutes later, Lindsay jumped to her feet. Garth was gone.

"Not in the apartment," Anna said after she'd checked the bedrooms.

They looked through the hall and downstairs and searched the courtyard and Lindsay's apartment. "Not again!" Lindsay said. But just as they were ready to start checking the streets for him, Garth showed up in the lobby.

"Where were you?" Lindsay demanded.

"Kitty," Garth said.

"Garth, that's it! Now you're going to stay in your room for running away from me." Lindsay took his arm and began to march him off. Instantly he squatted so that she had to drag him. She picked him up.

"No," Garth said, kicking at her to get away. "Kitty's crying."

"You heard Toasty?" Anna asked him. Garth pointed up the stairs to Hogan's apartment.

"Come on. We'd better go see," Amesley said.

Lindsay hauled Garth up the stairs after the twins. Outside Hogan's door, they stopped to listen. Lindsay could hear a faint mewling.

"Sounds like the cat's in there all right," Amesley said. "But Hogan moved out."

"Maybe the cat didn't," Anna said. She tried the door. "Looks like Betty didn't get a chance to lock the place up yet." Anna opened the door.

To Lindsay's amazement, there was Sapphire, pitifully thin, crouched in the kitchen sink next to a dripping faucet. The bowls which Hogan had probably used to feed her were on the floor— empty. Next to them, ironically, was a stack of canned cat food and a can opener.

"Bro-ther," Amesley said. "Why didn't Hogan tell us the cat was in the apartment when he asked us to feed her?"

"How were we supposed to know he'd left Toasty in here?" Anna sounded indignant.

The minute Lindsay picked up Sapphire, who felt weightless in her arms, the cat began to purr. "We better get some food in her," Lindsay said as she rubbed behind Sapphire's ear.

The pool table and the couch were still in the living room, but the sleeping bag was gone and the apartment felt deserted. They were all very quiet as they watched Sapphire gobble down a can of food. "We better not give her any more on an empty stomach," Anna said.

"I bet Hogan thought he told us," Amesley said. "You know, in the note he left with the plant."

"I guess because he leaves the door unlocked—" Lindsay said.

"But what if Betty had come snooping around?" Anna said. "Toasty would have been safer outside on her own."

"Nah," Amesley said. "One whiff of Betty and that cat would've hid."

"Where?" Anna asked.

Their eyes fixed on the couch, which seemed to be the only possible hiding place. "Anyway, Betty didn't get to this apartment," Lindsay said. "Mr. Prior had his attack and she took care of him instead."

"I found Kitty," Garth said proudly. He had climbed up on the pool table and was walking around the felt top, poking his bare toes into the pockets.

"He's right," Anna said. "He did."

But seeing him, Lindsay recalled her duty. Garth needed disciplining. She said, "You were a bad boy to run away, Garth. How can I make you understand you can't just take off without telling me? You're going to have to stay in our apartment today. Come on." She lifted him down.

"Hey," Amesley said. "He saved the cat's life. She would've starved to death if Garth hadn't found her."

Garth grinned his twisted grin at Lindsay hopefully. "That's true," she said. "But he still took off without letting me know. I can't keep letting him get away with that."

Just as Anna and Amesley exchanged a surprised look, Garth pulled loose from Lindsay. Before he could scoot out the door, she tackled him and lugged him down to their apartment while he yelled in protest.

A few minutes later, Anna knocked on the door to ask if Lindsay could take Toasty in. "We can't keep her. Ma claims our place is too small for us and pets, too," Anna said.

"We'd better leave Sapphire in Hogan's apartment then," Lindsay said, "because my mother would make us tell Betty we've found her cat."

"Rats," Anna said.

"Why don't we just let Sapphire run loose? She can hide in the tree and we can feed her," Lindsay suggested.

"Except if that catcatcher kid comes back," Anna said.

They decided to leave the cat in Hogan's apartment until the next morning, when it might be safer to release her. Lindsay was just about to invite Anna to come in and play a game when she said abruptly, "See you later," and left.

What did Anna have to do now that was so important, Lindsay wondered. True, Anna was too old to be her friend and kind of a know-it-all besides. But Lindsay was still sorry she had taken off so fast.

❧

That evening Lindsay saw Betty pass through the courtyard and return from Mr. Prior's apartment with a small airline carry-on bag. "How's Mr. Prior doing?" Lindsay called from her window.

Betty located where the voice was coming from and stopped to answer. "Fortunately it was just a mild heart attack. However, I'm the only one who may see him as yet. And when he's released in a couple of days, I intend to bring him to my house because, of course, he can't return to his apartment alone."

Betty's smile seemed smug to Lindsay. It was as if capturing at least one of the creatures she'd been pursuing had pleased Betty very much indeed.

chapter

$$\boxed{12}$$

The catcatcher was sitting in his chair by eight o'clock the next morning. This time he had come equipped with a bottle of water and a brown paper bag.

"We can't let Sapphire out with him here, can we?" Lindsay whispered to the twins who had met her and Garth in the courtyard.

"Right, but Hogan's apartment's beginning to stink," Amesley said. "That cat's not potty-trained to use the toilet."

"I'll clean up," Lindsay offered. Having cleaned up after ponies and horses and rabbits, she didn't expect cat waste to bother her.

An idea popped into her head and she asked, "What about Hogan? Maybe he could take Sapphire to wherever he's living now."

"Hey, yeah," Amesley said. "Let's go over to the car wash and ask him."

Anna balked immediately. "That man makes my skin crawl," she said. "You two go ahead, and I'll take Garth to the playground."

Lindsay hesitated.

"Don't worry, I baby-sit kids worse than him. He won't give me any trouble," Anna assured her.

Garth eyed Anna suspiciously. "Go see Hogan," he muttered.

"Thanks, Anna, but Garth should stay with me," Lindsay said. She didn't like Anna talking about Garth as if he were a troublemaker. "Anyway, Hogan likes Garth. It might help to have him along."

"Suit yourself," Anna said huffily. "I guess I'll start for the playground alone, then." She turned to her brother and said, "But you better get there right after you talk to Hogan, or I'll tell Ma."

Amesley ignored her threat. "Come on, short stuff. Let's cruise." He took Garth's hand and set off so fast that Garth had to run to keep up. So did Lindsay.

The dingy street seemed to be blinking sleepily in the hazy morning light. A dog on a leash lifted its leg against some garbage cans while its owner pretended not to notice. "Used to be drugs sold on this corner after school," Amesley said, "but the police stopped that pretty good."

Amesley detoured a block to show Lindsay the old elementary school he and Anna had attended before the building had been closed. It had neither grass nor a paved yard for kids to play in. From a distance it looked to Lindsay like a prison built of stone blocks. She would have hated to go there, or for Garth to go there if he were ready for school.

"What did you do for recess?" she asked.

"We didn't have any," Amesley said. "We had a gym. No cafeteria, though. Kids went home for lunch. Now kids around here get bused to a school with a ball field and a playground and a cafeteria. Not bad, huh?"

Lindsay watched a pigeon sailing wide-winged overhead. "I like school," she said, "if the teacher's nice."

"Yeah," Amesley said. "And if you get to play ball." Crossing the main avenue, they nearly got hit by a bare-chested teen ager gleaming with sweat who pedaled his bicycle furiously past them. When they reached the sidewalk, Amesley said, "Anna can get to be a pain sometimes. I guess you found that out?"

Lindsay shrugged. She didn't want to admit that she'd begun not to like Anna much.

"But you know, she means things for your own good. Like that trial? She was just trying to make you see that it wasn't your fault. We weren't being mean. I mean, we didn't mean to be mean, if you know what I mean."

Lindsay laughed. "I know that, Amesley. But

Anna does get me mad sometimes because she's so—"

"Bossy. Yeah. That's why she doesn't have any friends. You gotta be tough to stand up to Anna."

It shocked Lindsay to hear that Anna was friendless. She couldn't think of anything worse than not having a friend. "Does she mind?" Lindsay asked. "I mean, not having anybody?"

"Oh, sure. It gets to her and she cries. But like I tell her, it's her own fault."

Poor Anna, Lindsay thought as they approached the car wash. She would never have guessed that Anna's hard shell hid such softness. Out of sympathy for an easily hurt Anna, Lindsay said, "Mostly her ideas are good, though."

"Yeah," Amesley agreed. "Like I notice you've been keeping short stuff on a tight leash since that trial." He grinned down at his little buddy who grinned back happily.

"That's not because of the trial," Lindsay said. "I just made up my mind he's got to behave." The words weren't out of her mouth before she asked herself, Is that true? She hadn't been successful getting Garth to behave before the trial. Had it been Anna, then, Anna and her trial, that made the difference? Something had made a difference. Amesley was right about that.

". . . Yeah," Amesley was saying. "Anna's good at shaking people up."

Anna was such a mix of good and bad traits that it was hard to figure out how to feel about her, Lindsay was thinking. Right now she was inclined to like Anna again. Anna was a little like Jill, whose chatter and pushiness got on Lindsay's nerves, but who could be great fun sometimes. Rona was the only girl Lindsay knew who didn't have any faults. . . . Except Rona did forget to return things she borrowed, and sometimes she could get pretty grouchy. And those were faults, weren't they? Little faults, but still . . .

Lindsay wondered if Anna would want to be her friend despite the difference in their ages. Maybe she would since she didn't have a lot of other choices.

Hogan was drying the dripping sides of a car that had just emerged from the car wash when they reached him. "Hi, Hogan, how's it going?" Amesley called.

Hogan turned in a crouch, frowning in blank-faced confusion at the three of them.

"You remember us? From the apartment house," Amesley said.

"I got to work," Hogan mumbled. Toweling off the car vigorously, he dried it fast. It took off, but no other rolled out from the car wash for his attention.

"We wanted to ask you a favor. It's about the cat," Lindsay said. Deliberately she used his name for Sapphire. "You know, Raki?"

"Got to work." Hogan sank his head into his shoulders as if to hide. He began easing himself into the open maw of the car wash, where the felt fingers hung down like strange leaves in a dark tropical jungle.

Garth caught Hogan's leg before he got very far. "Hi," Garth said. Confidently he tipped his face up at his friend, showing his scar-mangled smile below sky-blue eyes and sunny curls.

Hogan focused on Garth as if the child mesmerized him.

"I found Kitty," Garth said proudly.

"Yeah?"

"Kitty was hungry."

"Listen, Mr. Hogan," Lindsay interrupted to say, "can you take Raki to your new apartment for a while? Because the landlady has a kid sitting in the courtyard to catch her, and if Raki stays around our building—well, you know."

"Betty's threatening to have her put down," Amesley said bluntly.

"Old, sharp-nosed witch," Hogan said, tensing with instant anger. "Thinks I'm going to pay rent for her stinkhole when the toilet don't even work. Who needs that place? I can sleep anywheres for free in the summer."

"Did you move to someplace near here?" Lindsay asked.

Hogan glanced at her sullenly, then turned his

head away. "The cat can stay in my room," he said. "Rent's paid till the end of the month."

"But Raki doesn't like being indoors," Lindsay said.

"And if we let her out, that kid'll catch her," Amesley said.

Hogan shook his head. "What do you want from me? Leave me alone. I can't do nothing. Can't do nothing for nobody." He looked at Garth and said softly, "Go away, kid. Go away." Then he ducked into the car wash.

"Do you think he doesn't *have* another apartment?" Lindsay asked.

Amesley sniffed. "Bet you he's sleeping in the park. But I don't see why when his rent's paid up until August."

"He probably just doesn't want anything to do with Betty."

"Yeah, well, who would?" Amesley said. "So now we gotta think of some other place for the cat."

"You have friends, Amesley," Lindsay said.

"Not in this neighborhood. Ma won't let Anna and me make friends here. In school I've got friends, but I don't know where they live."

"I guess we'll have to keep Sapphire in Hogan's apartment, then."

"Yeah, that's probably the best we can do."

"But suppose Betty goes in there?"

"She won't. Not while she's busy taking care of Mr. Prior," Amesley said. He flexed his muscles and stretched his back. "What we oughta do is get some cat litter so that Betty can't claim Hogan stunk up the place and keep his two-month rental deposit on him."

When they got back, Amesley talked Anna into lending him enough money from her hoard of saved allowances to buy a bag of litter. He went off to get it while Lindsay set about cleaning up Hogan's apartment. She couldn't get the pungent odor of cat urine out entirely, even though she scrubbed the bathroom and sprayed it with Mama's can of disinfectant.

Meanwhile Garth bounced on Hogan's couch and Sapphire rubbed against Lindsay's arms and tickled her chin with her dark, twitchy tail. When Lindsay persisted in scrubbing instead of playing with her, Sapphire reached out a paw, claws retracted, and pushed Lindsay's arm. "Merrow?" she invited Lindsay. "Merrow?" Then she thrust her narrow head, blue eyes open and innocent as Garth's, close to Lindsay's face.

"You're a love," Lindsay told the cat. She took Sapphire into her arms and cuddled her, pleased with the cat's contented purr.

Garth came over and leaned his cheek against Sapphire's back where the fur was the color of coffee. "Hi, Kitty," he said, tapping her gently.

Anna walked in then. She dumped the litter Amesley had bought in a box she'd lined with a plastic shopping bag. "I hope Toasty knows what this is for," Anna said.

"Sapphire's a smart cat," Lindsay assured her. "And she did live in a house when Betty's sister was alive."

Garth offered Sapphire a ball from the pool table. Immediately she jumped from Lindsay's arms to bat the ball around the floor. When she wearied of the ball, she wove herself around their ankles, accepting their tribute with a regal air as they told her, "You're so pretty . . . so cute . . . what a love." Their fingers trailed gently over her head every time she passed close to one of them. In a minute, she got bored with being admired and skittered away to stalk a fly.

She seemed content to stay when they left the apartment, but before they were halfway down the stairs, she began yowling her protest at being deserted again.

"Uh-oh, if Betty's catcatcher hears that, Toasty's done for," Anna said in the hallway.

"I've got some yarn in my bear box," Lindsay said. "Maybe if she had more to play with, she wouldn't be so bored."

"Bear box?" Anna questioned. Lindsay took her downstairs to show her the collection of three-inch-high bears.

"I was planning on making lots more costumes for them to show at the 4-H club exhibit at the county fair this summer," Lindsay said. "See, this one I started was going to be a drummer."

"You could make the whole band," Anna said. "I've got some gold piping you could use for braid. I'd help you . . . If you want." Anna said the last stiffly and looked away from Lindsay as if she didn't care one way or the other. But thanks to what Amesley had told her, Lindsay wasn't deceived.

"That'd be nice," she said. "You know what? We could sew in Hogan's place and keep Sapphire company."

"Let's do that," Anna said. They passed the afternoon happily, snipping and sewing tiny hats and red jackets. For the musical instruments they used shelf paper with a wood design on it that Lindsay had. Amesley brought over his box of plastic figures to keep Garth busy. The cat played with a curl of ribbon for a while, then coiled nose-to-tail in Lindsay's bear box on top of her sewing supplies and went to sleep.

This time when they left her, Sapphire didn't cry.

"If Betty takes Mr. Prior to her house from the hospital, that'll keep her too busy to come here, don't you think?" Lindsay asked hopefully in the dingy lobby.

"Yeah," Amesley said. "But I feel sorry for Mr. Prior, having to let that old lady take care of him."

"Well, they used to be sweethearts," Lindsay said. "So maybe he'll like her fussing over him."

"Wanna bet?" Amesley said.

Nobody did.

"That cat's just got to be lucky," Anna said. "Nothing else we can do for her."

❧

In bed that night, Lindsay thought, two days more and it would be Saturday and she'd be seeing Rona in Schuylerville. What would Rona have gotten her for a birthday present? Figuring out what to get each other was always a big deal for her and Rona and Jill. It took hours of secret telephone conferences to decide on something unique and not too expensive for the birthday girl. An animal poster was usually a safe bet for Lindsay, and Jill loved unicorns. For Rona, it had to be something practical, like a T-shirt or a fancy hair clip.

But the presents didn't matter. Just being with Rona for a day was going to be wonderful, not to mention the miniature golf and lunch treat. Lindsay could hardly wait.

chapter

13

The phone rang as Mama was about to leave for work the next morning. "Yes, Dr. Markowitz. Yes, Doctor," Mama kept saying. And then she said, "That's really nice. We appreciate that you— Yes, we'll be waiting for your call. Yes. Thank you." She sounded happy, but after she hung up and looked at Lindsay, the joy on her face slid into sorrow.

"What is it, Mama?"

"Well, it's good for Garth but bad for you. There's a friend of Dr. Markowitz—some famous plastic surgeon—coming to visit him this weekend, and Dr. Markowitz got him to agree to see Garth and give us a free consultation about how to fix his face."

"But?"

"But we have to be ready to get over there whenever the doctor calls, which means we can't go to Schuylerville. Not this weekend."

"Oh," Lindsay said. "Oh." She wanted to cry. She wanted to scream. It wasn't fair. Her eyes filled with tears. She'd been so good. Didn't she deserve anything for taking care of Garth so well? And this was her birthday, her twelfth birthday. But . . . No, she told herself after the first wave of disappointment crashed over her. No, it *was* fair. Because she'd let Garth go, hadn't she? If she'd held on to him that day, he wouldn't need a plastic surgeon. In a way, the famous doctor was a gift for her, too.

She took a deep breath and said, "It's okay, Mama. I understand."

Quickly Mama said, "We can do the party next weekend. Okay?"

"Sure," Lindsay said without enthusiasm. A belated birthday party wasn't the same thing. But— and she said it aloud this time—"It's only fair. It's my fault Garth got bashed."

"What?" Mama looked shocked. "Lindsay, what do you mean? What happened to Garth wasn't your fault. Whatever gave you that idea?"

"I was the one who let go of him," Lindsay said patiently. "I was the one supposed to be watching him."

"But you shouldn't have been. He's my responsibility, your father's and my responsibility, not yours. You're just a child. Anyway, the whole thing was an accident. And if anyone was at fault, it wasn't you. Oh, Lindsay!" Mama put her arms around

Lindsay and hugged her close. "Have you been thinking you did something wrong all this time?"

"It was an accident," Lindsay said, "but if I'd held him tighter—"

"No," Mama said. "Don't feel guilty about something you couldn't help. You should have told me that's what you were thinking. Why didn't you?"

Lindsay shrugged. "Because—" She thought of how it had been after Garth's accident, Mama hysterical and crying while she cooked and cleaned and drove to the hospital to visit Garth, and Dad so distraught he went around muttering to himself. Neither of them had lashed out at Lindsay. In fact they'd told her it wasn't her fault. But she hadn't believed them. She'd crept unobtrusively through the days, too smothered in guilt to think or feel, aware only of the hurtful beating of her heart.

Mama's eyes blurred with tears. "*I* know," she said. "*I* know. You're just like me. You keep everything inside. Bud says it's better to talk it out. I can't, though. I never could. But you're young enough to learn." Mama shook Lindsay's shoulders as if to shake what she was saying into her. "Lindsay, believe me, it's better to let it out."

Dad had a late class that morning so he was still in the bathroom. When he came out and Mama told him about the special doctor, Dad said, "You know what we can do? We can celebrate your birthday tomorrow night, Lindsay. We'll bring in pizza and blow up balloons and have a party just for us."

She nodded, but then she had a sudden idea. "Could I invite some people from the house to have pizza with us?" she asked.

"Sure," Dad said. He raised an eyebrow. "But who'd you invite?"

"Well, Anna and Amesley have been good to me." Lindsay smiled. "And Sapphire—she's a cat so she won't eat much pizza."

Dad laughed. "That's my honey girl. You're some great kid, you know that?" His hug squeezed the breath out of her.

"Where is that cat?" Mama asked. "I haven't seen her around lately."

"We've been hiding her from Betty. Betty's hired a boy to trap her. She's going to have Sapphire put to sleep."

"Oh, no!" Mama said. "Surely Betty wouldn't do that to such a beautiful animal."

"Well, Sapphire scratched her a little. She scratched Garth and me, too, but not much. Betty thinks that means the cat's gone wild."

"So that was where Garth got hurt," Mama said. "Garth told me it was from playing."

"Could we keep Sapphire in our apartment, Mama?" Lindsay asked. "It'd be safer for her."

"I couldn't do that," Mama said. "Hide the land-lady's cat? No, that would be wrong."

"Cats are pretty good at taking care of themselves, Lindsay," Dad said. "Besides, old Betty's probably just bluffing."

"I'll get invitations, Lindsay," Mama said. "And you can ask anyone you want and decorate the living room."

"And then I get to see Rona next week?" Lindsay asked.

"Sure," Dad said. "Now that's not a bad deal, is it? Two parties instead of one?"

Lindsay nodded, but she was thinking about Sapphire and wondering if he was right. Had Betty been bluffing? Would the cat survive even if she did get caught?

Lindsay dreaded calling Rona, but all Rona said was that getting together a week later would be fine. Her father had her busy refilling the vegetable displays at the food stand, and he was paying her. "I'm going to be rich by the end of the summer, Lindsay. I'm going to buy myself a new bike," Rona said. She told Lindsay about the postcard from Jill that she could hardly read because Jill wrote so small and so much.

"How's that girl?" Lindsay asked. "The one who moved into my house?"

"Okay. I had lunch there yesterday. She has your bedroom, Lindsay, but she didn't fix it up nearly as nice as you did."

Lindsay was jealous. It seemed that the new girl

was getting her old friend as well as her old house. Regretfully Lindsay remembered the bedroom window from which she had seen the deer at the salt lick last winter and heard the red-winged blackbirds singing this spring after the snow melted. The courtyard was tight as a trap compared to the sweep of that field, which went all the way to the woodlot a quarter of a mile off.

"Anything new with you?" Rona asked her. And Lindsay told her about the specialist who was going to look at Garth's face. "That's great, Lindsay. I hope he figures out how to fix it like new." Rona's voice was creamy with sympathy. She understood that the accident had devastated Lindsay.

But then Rona said, "So is Garth still giving you a hard time?"

"What do you mean? Garth's a good kid," Lindsay said. "And lately he's really been listening to me."

"Yeah, well, he's past due to outgrow the terrible twos."

Lindsay knew Garth's changed behavior was more than just outgrowing a phase, but she wasn't about to go into it over the phone. Too much had happened, too many subtle details that were hard to explain.

"Have you made friends yet?" Rona asked.

"Sort of," Lindsay said. "There's twins, Amesley and Anna. They're thirteen but they're very nice.

And Mr. Prior. He's pretty old and he had a heart attack, but he's coming out of the hospital."

"Weird!" Rona said. "You're hanging out with an old man and a boy and a girl who're so much older than you? You must be pretty desperate, Lindsay."

Instead of mentioning that her other companion was a cat, Lindsay said, "See you on the Saturday after this, Rona," and left it at that. Mama had gone off to work while Lindsay was on the phone. Garth had taken the big bottle of orange juice from the refrigerator and was pouring juice into his plastic cup and onto the floor.

"Garth, let me pour that for you," Lindsay said.

Obediently he handed her the jar. "Sorry," he said looking at the spreading puddle. "I clean up."

She was so pleased that he was finally taking responsibility for what he had done that she gave him the dishrag and let him slop it around the floor until he got tired. When he said, "All done," and returned to the TV, she finished the wipe-up job, smiling to herself.

Lindsay had just gotten dressed when she heard the toilet flushing. The continuous flushing sounded wrong. She hustled to the bathroom to find Garth squatting naked in the toilet, flushing the water over his legs and bottom.

He looked so funny it was hard not to laugh. "The toilet's to go potty in, Garth. You shouldn't waste water by playing in it. And anyway, you're making it overflow."

150

"You're mean," he said.

"Me? I'm a good sister." She hoisted him out of the toilet and began to dry him off. "And you're going to be a good brother, right?" She kissed his pudgy nose, thinking that it would be wonderful when the scars were erased and he looked like his old self.

"I'm good," he said.

"Are you? Then how about showing me how good you can be today?"

"Okay," he agreed.

And to her surprise he did behave himself. He even asked her if he could have another cookie after lunch instead of sneaking the box off the shelf and gobbling up as many as he could before she caught him.

Early in the afternoon, Lindsay was surprised to see Mr. Prior sitting on his bench under the tree dressed in his usual sport coat and shirt. He didn't look much paler than he had before he went into the hospital.

"Mr. Prior!" she yelled. In her excitement, she took a shortcut out the window, lifting Garth over the sill after her onto the split-open bags of leaves still piled there. "How are you? I'm so glad you're back."

"I'm not quite back, Lindsay. I've been released from the hospital into Betty's care. She's just packing up some essentials for my stay at her house." Mr. Prior turned to greet Garth in his usual courteous way, but Garth had spotted his pail and shovel near the hedge and trotted off to reclaim them.

"Your lovely get-well card cheered me immensely, Lindsay. Thank you. You made this old man feel wanted," Mr. Prior said.

"We had fun making the cards," Lindsay said absently. Something else was on her mind. "Mr. Prior? Will you live at Betty's for good?"

Mr. Prior's mouth curled upward and his narrow eyes twinkled under their heavy lids. "Not if I can help it," he confided. "As soon as I'm strong enough to manage, I plan to return to my solitary bachelor existence. Betty means well, but I'm too old for a bib and highchair."

Lindsay was relieved to hear it. "Good," she said. Then she told him how they were keeping Sapphire locked up in Hogan's apartment and only letting her out at night to avoid Betty's catcatcher. "But Hogan's rent is just paid up till the end of the month, and we don't know where to hide Sapphire after that," Lindsay said.

"Aha! Sounds as if you need me back in the cat conspiracy." Mr. Prior sounded glad of it. "Let me think about what we can do next."

"Could you keep Betty from putting Sapphire down if she catches her?"

"I can try. That's the least I can do for the cat and a good friend like you, Lindsay." He nodded as usual, as if agreeing with himself.

His friend, he had called her. While Lindsay filled in the hole Garth had redug in the soft dirt where he usually played, she determined that *her* friend, Mr. Prior, should also have an invitation to the birthday party.

Mama brought home a pack of eight invitations illustrated with a child in a birthday hat eating an ice-cream cone. Lindsay immediately sat down and wrote out one each to Amesley and Anna and Mr. Prior. That left five. She went to the stove where Mama was cooking chili, helped by Garth, who was standing on a stool beside her and stirring.

"Mama, would it be okay if I asked Hogan to come? I know he's a little strange, but Garth likes him. And Hogan was the one who took care of Sapphire most."

"You can ask him, but he probably won't come. Lindsay, if you want me to deliver the invitation to Mr. Prior at Betty's house, maybe you ought to invite her, too—just to be polite."

"Betty! But I don't like her, Mama. And if she comes, I can't have Sapphire."

"Well, don't invite her then, but maybe you shouldn't invite Mr. Prior, either. Otherwise you'll hurt her feelings. Think about it," Mama said when Lindsay was silent.

Unable to make up her mind what to do about Mr. Prior and Betty, Lindsay made out an invitation for Garth and gave it to him. "I'll come," he said, pretending to read it. "Did you invite Kitty?"

She wrote out an invitation for Sapphire just for fun, and then she said, "Oops, I forgot to invite the twins' mother." Writing that one took care of all the invitations except the one Mama wanted her to make out for Betty. Lindsay set that aside with Mr. Prior's in case she changed her mind and decided to invite them both. In big letters at the bottom of all the cards Lindsay wrote, "R.S.V.P. and no presents, please."

Mama had the morning off. She said it was funny that on her time away from the post office, Lindsay was keeping her busy delivering mail. First they gave the Blakes their invitations, and then Mama walked with Lindsay and Garth to the car wash to deliver Hogan's.

He looked anxious when Lindsay put the square envelope in his hand. "What's this?" he asked Lindsay.

"An invitation to my birthday party," she said. "We're going to have pizza and ice cream. Everybody in the apartment house is invited. I hope you can come. It's this evening."

Hogan stared at the envelope before he opened it. Then he stared at the card, turning it over to examine the back. Finally he read the inside.

"You know which apartment I live in, don't you, Hogan?" Lindsay asked because he looked so confused.

"By the big plastic bags," Garth said helpfully.

Shyly Hogan's eyes found Lindsay's face. "It's not a joke?"

"No," she said.

"Nobody ever invited me to their birthday party before," he muttered without looking at her.

Lindsay bit her lip, feeling bad for him. When he didn't say anything more, she finally said, "Well, I hope you'll come."

A driver honked impatiently for Hogan's attention. Carefully Hogan slid the envelope into his shirt pocket. Then he bent to his work.

Lindsay and her mother swung Garth between them most of the way home.

"I think your Mr. Hogan really liked getting that invitation," Mama said. "Maybe he will come after all."

"I hope so," Lindsay said. She was concerned about whether he had understood the no-present rule because she didn't think he had much money. "You can't earn a lot drying cars, can you, Mama?"

"Not much," Mama said. "What will you do about Mr. Prior and Betty?"

"I don't know yet."

Disaster struck that afternoon when Mama was back at work. Lindsay was blowing up balloons to hang from the streamers Mama had crisscrossed on the living room ceiling. It was hot and the living room window was open. Nobody was in the courtyard. Garth was batting a blue balloon around the floor and Sapphire, whom Lindsay had released from Hogan's apartment, was stalking it. Garth pushed the balloon out the window into the courtyard, and when Sapphire leaped after it, he clapped his hands and chortled. A second later he yelled, "No!" and began scrambling out the window himself.

Not again, Lindsay thought. She finished tying off a balloon, then followed her brother out the window. To her horror, she saw the catcatching boy in the courtyard. He gave a yell of triumph as he shoved a struggling Sapphire into Betty's cage. Before he could get through the gate, though, the balloon popped and Garth bit his leg. The startled boy raised his hand to defend himself.

"Don't you hit my brother," Lindsay said. She leaped from the pile of bags and ran to the rescue. The boy shook Garth off and escaped into the street with Sapphire yowling eerily from the cage.

Lindsay shook with cold despair. Why did things have to go bad again just when they seemed to be getting better? Now Sapphire was lost.

Unless Mr. Prior could keep Betty from having the cat put down. Or unless Lindsay could think of a way to save her.

chapter

14

The catcatcher's awful yell of triumph when he trapped Sapphire kept echoing in Lindsay's head. She stood in her streamer-bedecked living room, where the breeze was playfully bumping balloons about, trying to think of a way to save the cat.

Mr. Prior couldn't do it alone, weak as he was from his hospital stay. What if Betty were invited to the birthday party tonight and all her tenants were there and they backed Mr. Prior up? Would that make Betty change her mind? Maybe not. She probably didn't much care what her tenants thought about her. But if she cared even a little— Anyway, it was the only idea Lindsay had.

It took her less than a minute to write out the invitation. The problem was where to deliver it. Mama had Betty's address, but Mama was at work. The Blakes must know, too. Yes, Amesley would know.

Lindsay set off to the playground with Garth and the invitations to find Amesley. Let Sapphire still be alive, Lindsay prayed. Don't let Betty have taken her to the vet to be put down.

Garth stooped to pet a cat sunning itself in a doorway. "We have to hurry, Garth," Lindsay said and pulled him along.

What if Betty was insulted at being invited on such short notice and wouldn't come and wouldn't let Mr. Prior go without her? What if Amesley and Anna and Garth were the only party guests? Ms. Blake had already stopped by to say she had taken a part-time job waitressing on weekend evenings and was sorry she couldn't be there tonight. Hogan wasn't likely to show. Dad wouldn't be home until late. Glumly, Lindsay hoped Mama didn't get too much pizza.

Amesley was on the ball field waiting for his turn at bat when Lindsay approached him. As soon as she'd explained why she was there, he dropped his bat and told the other ballplayers he'd see them later. "Hey, Anna," he yelled at his sister who was lost in a book as usual. "We gotta go someplace. Come on."

Anna didn't budge until they'd told her what was so urgent. Then Amesley hoisted Garth onto his shoulders and the three of them set off for the tree-lined street where Betty lived. Her big Victorian house was the lone single-family residence among the parking lots and funeral parlors.

Even the ten-foot-high fence and gigantic hedges surrounding the house couldn't hide it from the street.

Anna stopped on the sidewalk in front of the fancy wrought-iron gate.

"I don't want to go in there," she said.

The house dismayed Lindsay, too, but when she saw Amesley was also hesitating, she said, "I'll knock. Betty's not so bad."

"Yeah?" Amesley said. "Who says?"

"Who says?" Garth echoed, his chin on Amesley's head.

"Mr. Prior," Lindsay told them.

Amesley wrinkled his nose in doubt. "Well, go on, then, and me and short stuff'll follow you."

Silently Anna fell into place at the end of the line. Lindsay rang the doorbell.

"Hi," she said breathlessly when Betty answered the door.

"Yes?"

"I came to find out if you and Mr. Prior would like to come to my party this evening. With Sapphire," Lindsay blurted out and thrust the three small envelopes at the landlady.

Betty cleared her throat. "A party? Tonight? Well, I don't know." She put her finger to her lips, hesitating. "Why don't you wait a minute and I'll ask Stuart if he feels up to an excursion." Then she actually smiled at Lindsay, revealing, at long last, a trace of the charm Mr. Prior claimed she'd had as a young woman.

"Ask her how Sapphire is when she comes back," Anna whispered.

"I'll ask her," Amesley said. He was still carrying Garth, who now patted his cheek fondly.

They didn't have long to wait. Betty returned, smiling broadly now. "Stuart said he'd be delighted to attend your party. And since I certainly can't let him go anywhere alone, we'll both be coming."

"And Sapphire?" Amesley asked.

"I don't know about the cat," Betty said.

Lindsay's eyes filled with tears. "Please," she said. "Sapphire's my friend, too, and I'd like to have all my friends from the house."

"Well, that's dear of you, but—" Betty's polished pink nails touched her lips again.

"I could come and carry the cage for you," Amesley offered quickly. "And I'll carry it back, too, after the party."

"Thank you but that's not necessary," Betty said. "I'll have to hire a taxi to bring us there and home anyway. However, I doubt that the driver would be willing to take an animal in his cab."

"Oh, sure he will," Amesley said. "Those guys take people with pets to the vet all the time. And you got the cage to carry her in. So no problem."

"No problem," Garth parroted from his perch.

Betty pursed her lips at Garth. "Yes, well, we'll

see. I have to go now. It's time for Stuart's medicine."

From somewhere in the house came the plaintive "Meerowwww" of a cat being held against its will. Four heads turned toward the sound just as the door shut them out.

"Sapphire's still alive!" Lindsay exulted.

"Whew!" Amesley said. "That's as nice as I ever heard that old witch talk. I guess she's feeling good 'cause she's got hold of Mr. Prior *and* her sister's cat. How come you didn't say boo, Anna?"

Anna grunted.

"Cat got your tongue?" Amesley teased.

"Oh, shut up, Amesley. You weren't so brave," Anna said. "If Lindsay hadn't gone first, you wouldn't have rung that bell."

"Who says?" Amesley blustered.

Garth put his hands over Amesley's eyes and said, "Giddyap, Amesley."

"Giddyap yourself, short stuff." Amesley swung Garth down in one smooth motion and challenged him to a race. The two of them set off for home, Garth's legs churning fast while Amesley ran in slow motion.

"Amesley thinks he's so tough!" Anna said.

"If only we could make Betty like the cat," Lindsay said.

"We'll think of something," Anna said. "You were pretty quick coming up with what to say at the door. And Mr. Prior'll be there to help us."

Surely Betty wasn't more powerful than all of them together, Lindsay thought hopefully. Surely they could persuade her.

⚜

At four o'clock Lindsay created a table centerpiece with the marching band of bears she and Anna had made. The ice cream was already in the freezer. Somehow Mama had found time before she left for work at noon to bake a birthday cake with Lindsay's name on it. The cake was in the refrigerator now, along with three big bottles of soda, both diet and regular cola and one orange soda.

At five Mama came home with a stack of boxed pizzas and set them in the oven to warm. "Happy, happy birthday, Lindsay," she said. She gave Lindsay a small kiss and a big bag of potato chips to empty into a bowl.

"Everybody's coming," Lindsay told her. When she finished explaining how that had come about, nothing remained to do but fidget and wait for her guests. "I hope Betty brings the cat," she kept saying until Mama told her to relax and stop thinking about it.

Garth was busy batting a couple of extra balloons around the living room when Lindsay let Anna and Amesley in. "Presents for me?" Garth asked when he saw the wrapped packages Anna and Amesley were carrying.

163

"Your sister's the birthday girl," Anna said.

"But I said not to bring any presents," Lindsay protested.

"These are no big deal," Anna said. "Anyway, mine isn't."

"Open them," Amesley said eagerly.

"Now?"

"Why not?"

She sat down and tore off the Sunday-comics wrapping on the bigger package, which turned out to be a bag of leather scraps in several colors.

"To make stuff for your bears," Anna said.

Lindsay enthused about what a great present it was while Amesley danced around waiting for her to open his package. "I spent my own money on it," he boasted.

"Oh, it's beautiful!" she told him when she'd unwrapped a large black china cat with painted turquoise eyes.

"I got it from the used furniture store. I figured you'd like it," Amesley said.

"I love it," Lindsay assured him.

The next guest to arrive was Hogan. He had also ignored the no-present request and was carrying a package almost as big as Garth.

"Oh, you shouldn't have!" Lindsay cried and meant it.

"Open it," Amesley said. "Don't you want her to open it, Hogan?"

"I didn't know what to get," he muttered, anxiously rubbing one hand with the other.

"Open it, Lindsay," Mama said. Her eyes warned Lindsay to make a fuss over it no matter what it was, a reminder Lindsay didn't need.

She took the wrapping paper off with a care that made Amesley groan. "Girls! What you want to save the wrapping paper for?"

"To wrap your present when it's your birthday, stupid," Anna said. Anna helped Lindsay undo the taped parts without ripping the pink tissue paper much. Inside the paper was a white fur cushion in the shape of a curled-up cat.

"Oh, it's gorgeous!" Lindsay squealed. She got up as if she meant to throw her arms around Hogan. Hastily he backed away from her. "Thanks, Hogan," she said. "But it's too much. You shouldn't have gotten me any present, and this is such a beautiful one. Thanks, Hogan."

It was the first time Lindsay had ever seen Hogan's smile. He was missing a lot of teeth for a man no older than her father. "I didn't know what to get," he repeated. This time he sounded proud of himself. His present had been a success.

By then it was after six. "I don't think Betty's bringing Mr. Prior and Sapphire," Lindsay fretted.

"Doesn't look like it," Mama said. "We'd better eat the pizza now."

Everybody sat down around the table. Lindsay

and Mama had borrowed chairs from the Blakes so there were enough to go around.

Just as Mama was dishing out the pizza, someone knocked on the door. Lindsay leaped to open it. There stood Mr. Prior lugging the cat carrier. Inside it was a crying Sapphire pressing her nose against the bars, frantic to get out. Garth pounced on the cage and unhooked the latch.

"Close the window, someone," Mama said. "We don't want to lose the landlady's cat."

"Where's Betty? Why didn't she come?" Lindsay asked.

Mr. Prior looked uncomfortable and glanced at Hogan. "She'll be here. She's attending to some business first."

Everyone made a big fuss over Mr. Prior, whom most of them hadn't seen since his heart attack had landed him in the hospital. He kept repeating, "It was nothing, nothing really. I'm fine." Lindsay ushered him to the couch and provided him with soda and pizza.

Mr. Prior looked around and said, "I see you've already received some birthday presents. Well, since I couldn't go shopping, the best I could do was to bring you one of my books. It's too young for you, I'm afraid, Lindsay, but I thought you might enjoy owning it." The book was about a gray striped cat, and Mr. Prior had drawn a picture of Sapphire on the flyleaf. "To my dear young friend, Lindsay, Many happy birthdays, Stuart Prior," he had written.

"Oh, Mr. Prior, I love it," Lindsay said. "I've never owned a book where I knew the author before. I'll keep it forever." When she hugged him, he flushed with pleasure and kissed her cheek.

Suddenly Sapphire jumped straight up out of the pile of boxes and wrapping paper in the middle of the living room floor. There were multiple squeals of surprise and laughter.

"I've heard of people bursting from cakes, but a cat is certainly special," Mr. Prior said.

"It's Sapphire's present to me," Lindsay said. She picked up the cat and cradled her in her arms. Sapphire looked up at her cross-eyed with her pink tongue stuck out.

Just then Betty arrived. She looked around the living room, which was strewn with presents and birthday wrappings, and said querulously, "Did everyone here bring you a present but me?"

Lindsay was embarrassed. "Well, nobody was supposed to."

"I brought her a china cat," Amesley said. He held it up so Betty could see it.

"I just brought her a bag of leather scraps to use for costumes," Anna said. "Hogan bought her the best gift." She pointed to the cat pillow.

Betty hadn't noticed Hogan before. He'd backed into the kitchen when she arrived. "What are *you* doing here?" she demanded.

"He's a friend of mine," Lindsay said.

"Is he indeed? Well, I've just inspected his

apartment—which was unlocked even though I'd warned you not to leave it that way, *Mr.* Hogan. And I may as well tell you, I'm not returning your security deposit. It will cost me at least that much to have the place fumigated."

"You old bag of—" Hogan began.

Instantly Lindsay grabbed his arm and interrupted him. "You mean that apartment still smells, Betty?" Lindsay said. "I tried to clean the cat smell. See, we were hiding Sapphire from you there because—Well, anyway, it wasn't Hogan's fault. He's very clean. The place didn't smell at all before we shut the cat in there. I'll scrub it some more tomorrow."

"*You* were hiding the cat from me?" Betty said to her. "Why that's—"

"We have all been involved in protecting the cat's independence," Mr. Prior said. "We didn't want to see her locked indoors after becoming such a liberated creature. She's used to coming and going at will now."

"Your sister's cat's neat," Amesley said. "Everybody in this house likes her. Hogan feeds her, and she sits on Mr. Prior's lap, and—"

"And you've all made an utter fool out of me," Betty snapped.

"Now, Betty," Mr. Prior said. "Aren't you pleased that your tenants are so congenial? And it's thanks to this creature. She's the spirit of the house as she flits about bestowing her affections on us." His fingers slipped over Sapphire as she stepped from the back of the couch to his shoulder and slid down his chest to his lap.

Betty seemed at a loss for words. She bit her lips and darted glances around the room. Distractedly she said, "I wish I'd known everyone was bringing presents. I certainly would have, but the invitation said—Well, there's no reason I can't give you a belated present, Lindsay. That's what I'll have to do."

"If you let Sapphire stay with us here in this apartment house, that'd be the best present you could give me," Lindsay said quickly.

Betty sighed. "It isn't wise to leave an animal in the charge of a group. Someone has to accept responsibility for it."

"Perhaps Lindsay would be willing to do that," Mr. Prior suggested as if it were a favor she might do for Betty.

Betty looked at Lindsay. "You wouldn't want to be responsible for the care of this cat, would you?"

"Oh, I would," Lindsay said. "That's all right, isn't it, Mama?"

"As far as I'm concerned," Mama said with a shy smile.

"The girl does seem to be fond of cats, doesn't she?" Betty said. Her eyes picked out the white cushion and the cat statue, as if it still bothered her that she hadn't brought a present.

169

"I love cats," Lindsay said. "Especially this one." She knelt to lay her cheek against Sapphire's coffee-and-cream side. A sandpapery tongue delicately licked Lindsay's nose.

"Of course," Mr. Prior said slyly, "you do have a rule about tenants not being allowed to keep pets, don't you, Betty?"

Betty straightened her small body importantly. "As the owner of this building, I can make exceptions to my own rules if I choose."

"That's true, my dear." Mr. Prior smiled his sweet turtle smile.

"As for you, Hogan," Betty said, "if you would only start locking your door, you could continue to rent the apartment as far as I'm concerned. I'll even have the toilet you complained about fixed."

Hogan looked at her with his jaw dropped open.

Betty nodded. "Well, then," she said, and she preened herself as if she were pleased with what she'd accomplished. "Is there any pizza left for me?"

Lindsay and Mama jumped to attend to their hostess duties. The sudden movement made Sapphire leap from Mr. Prior's lap into the pile of gift wrapping again.

"Kitty!" Garth cried and dove in after her.

Amesley ate six pieces of pizza. Garth shared his ice cream with the cat. Lindsay blew out all the candles on her cake. Afterward they played a card game called pig—even Garth played. Mr. Prior taught them the rules. The object was not to become the pig, who was the last person to put his finger on his nose after noticing the matched pair in the cards everyone turned over at the same time.

The biggest surprise was when Betty sang in a surprisingly young, sweet voice an old song about true love. She looked at Mr. Prior as she sang and he smiled at her in such a way that Lindsay wondered if he ever would declare himself well enough to return to his bachelor pad.

Hogan was the last one to leave. "I lost the key," he whispered to Lindsay. "You think she'd get me another one maybe, huh?"

"I'll ask her for you," Lindsay said, and thanked him again for his present.

"You know," she said dreamily to her mother when everyone had gone and they were cleaning up, "city living's kind of exciting."

"You certainly have made friends in a very short time," Mama said.

"Umm," Lindsay admitted. None of them were just like her, the way her friends in Schuylerville were. But Amesley and Anna and Mr. Prior were certainly sharing her life, and they cared about her and she liked them. That must make them friends, good friends in fact.

She looked at Sapphire, who was curled up next to Garth with all her brown tips interlaced. "Garth," she said. "You know what? You didn't give me a birthday present."

"I didn't?" He looked crushed. "What I give you?"

"How about a kiss?" She held her arms out. He made a running leap and gave her not only a kiss but a hug. His face was tipped up to grin at her and she looked at him without a twinge. It had been an accident, Mama said. Innocent, her friends had judged her. What had happened to Garth had just happened somehow. It wasn't her fault. She could love him with her whole heart the way she used to.

"Thanks, Garth," she said. "That was a really nice present."

Sapphire was asleep in the gift wrappings when Lindsay went to bed. It had been a remarkable birthday party, Lindsay thought, the most unusual she'd ever had. Maybe even the best.